Hox

Hox

Annemarie Allan

Kelpies

Kelpies is an imprint of Floris Books

This edition published in 2007 by Floris Books

The publisher acknowledges a Lottery grant from the Scottish Arts Council towards the publication of this series.

British Library CIP Data available

ISBN 978-086315-621-2

Produced in Poland by Polskabook

To Esme and her shoes

Chapter 1

"It's no good, Spike. You can't stay in here."

Robbie's Dad didn't like cats. He didn't really like any animals at all, which was odd considering the kind of work he did.

Robbie flicked an uneasy glance at the kitchen door as he grabbed a dishtowel and scrubbed at the muddy paw prints on the table. Spike yawned and rolled over to one side in a long, slow stretch.

Robbie understood perfectly. "I don't care how comfortable you are. You shouldn't be here. And neither should I," he muttered, thinking of the empty weekend ahead.

He lifted the cat and opened the back door. He could see next door's dog peering hopefully through the garden fence. Spike went rigid in his arms, but Robbie wasn't fooled. The dog was no threat. He was old and stiff and his bones ached too much in wet weather to care about anything except doing his business and getting back indoors as fast as possible.

"Go home, Spike." He dropped the cat on to the rain-soaked flagstones and stepped back into the house. "You don't want Dad to catch you in here."

The cat flicked his tail in a disdainful gesture and set off towards the bushes at the back of the garden just as Robbie's dad erupted into the kitchen.

"Don't be silly, Robbie! Why are you looking out there? Shut the door!"

Robbie did as he was asked. Michael Bruce looked around wildly.

"I've checked everywhere — they've got to be somewhere in the house. The car's still here after all." A shadow of doubt appeared on his father's bony face. "The car *is* here, isn't it?"

Robbie followed him into the hall. It was perfectly fine with him if the car keys didn't surface. He didn't like visiting the Institute. Not any more. He watched as his father pulled open the front door, peered outside, then rushed past on his way up the stairs.

"Maybe I left them in the bathroom. You check down here," he ordered.

While his father thundered from one room to another above his head, Robbie opened the door to the cupboard under the stairs. It was no surprise to see the car keys lying on the shelf next to the heating switch. Dad always put the heating on as soon as he came into the house.

He hesitated for a moment, tempted to say nothing. It would be a reasonable payback for his cancelled weekend. But it wasn't worth spending the next few minutes watching his father tear the house to pieces.

"Dad!" he yelled. "I found them. They're here!"

"Thanks, Robbie!" Michael ran downstairs and snatched them out of his hand, scooping up his briefcase on his way to the door. "Let's go. I'm supposed to be there in five minutes."

Robbie slouched in the passenger seat, eyes closed, trying to imagine he was on the road through Glencoe, driving across naked moorland towards distant, snow-capped mountains, instead of speeding along the main street of Duncraig while his father complained loudly about Saturday drivers, careless pedestrians and unco-operative traffic lights.

Robbie didn't open his eyes until he felt the car slow down and make a sharp left turn, through a pair of heavy metal gates, into the Institute for Animal Research. The security guard waved them in. For once, Robbie didn't wave back.

His father took a deep breath and smiled at Robbie. "Only a few minutes late after all. Thanks to you."

Robbie said nothing. Michael took one hand off the wheel and waved towards a small block of flats, just visible above the trees on the other side of a tall chain link fence.

"Do you remember when we lived over there? And you suddenly turned up in my office in the middle of the night in your pyjamas?"

But his clumsy attempt to lighten the atmosphere only reminded Robbie of how hard it was to get his father away from work for a single evening, let alone a whole weekend.

"I thought security was supposed to keep people out," he said. "It can't be much use if little kids can find their way in."

Michael glared at him. "There's nothing wrong with our security. We're not trying to find out if some deodorant gives you a rash, Robbie. You know we don't do that kind of work here. The animals have always been well cared for, not tortured."

Robbie glowered back as the car crunched its way up the gravel driveway.

"I don't see why you had to drag me here anyway. I'll just have to hang about for ages."

He stared straight ahead. There was nothing interesting to see. Only the solid grey bulk of the Institute. It had once been a private home, a massive Victorian mansion, with wide lawns at the front and a huge expanse of parkland at the back. Now it housed the offices and most of the Institute's laboratories.

"I thought you liked coming with me." His father looked at him with a puzzled frown as he turned towards the car park at the rear of the building.

Robbie sighed. "I'm twelve years old, Dad," he said. "I'm not a little kid any more." Then he stiffened and sat up straight. There it was again — just like last time. A tickle in his head, as though something was trying to worm its way inside.

His father stopped the car, reached into the back for his briefcase and climbed out. "I'll not be long."

"I should have gone to Ally's house. Then it really would be just like any other day." That was where Robbie usually ended up on school days when his father was going to be very late home.

"Alastair's away for the weekend," Michael reminded him. "And there's no one else."

"Lucky Ally," growled Robbie, wishing now that he had been invited along. But he didn't have that kind of relationship with Ally. Or with anyone else.

"Well, I can't leave you home alone all afternoon," said his father. "And if I get finished quickly enough, we might still have time to head off afterwards."

Robbie knew from experience how unlikely that was, but he wasn't interested in arguing about it. He was too busy trying to sort out the growing tension in his head.

His Dad's voice softened. "Please don't be awkward, Robbie. I've got no choice. You know that."

"It's me that's got no choice." He turned his head away and stared at the raindrops on the window. The sensation was much more than a tickle now. It was like someone knocking at the door to his mind, demanding to be let in.

The back door of the building swung open and Gavin Moir appeared at the top of the steps. Robbie didn't like him much. Moir was the Head of the Institute and he wasn't interested in talking to anyone who didn't matter. He usually looked through Robbie, as though he was invisible. Robbie watched him gesture impatiently, then tap his watch.

Michael Bruce waved back, and began to drum his fingers impatiently on the roof while Robbie undid his seatbelt and swung his feet out on to the gravel.

"Why don't you go and see Morag? She's got a really fancy graphics programme on her machine."

Morag was his father's latest student. She was the one who always got stuck with Robbie while Michael got on with what he needed to do. But Robbie wasn't really listening. He was concentrating on the feeling inside his head. It seemed to come and go like a radio signal, depending on which way he was facing. He stood up and turned his head, testing it out.

His father was waiting for an answer. He said the first thing that came into his head. “I think I’ll take a walk.”

“In the rain?”

Robbie shrugged. “I don’t mind.”

“Well, don’t go far. I’ll see you back here in about an hour.”

Robbie nodded. He watched his father cross the car park, climb the steps and bend his angular body to say something to Moir. But Gavin Moir wasn’t looking at Michael. For once, he was staring at Robbie ... and he looked angry. Maybe he thought it was Robbie’s fault that they were late. Or maybe people weren’t allowed to bring their children here any more. Dad was always complaining about how fussy people were getting about health and safety.

His mood lightening a little at the thought of how much it would annoy his father if Robbie couldn’t come to work with him anymore, he turned away and crunched across the gravel towards a tree-lined path.

When he looked back a minute later, both men had disappeared inside. Immediately, he changed direction, heading back along the side of the house, past a row of wheelie bins to the front of the building.

He stopped and stared at the barn-like structure hunched close to the ground on the other side of a smooth expanse of emerald lawn. It looked like a prison, with its heavy security door, shuttered windows covered in heavy-duty wire mesh and the chain link fence visible just behind it.

And that, thought Robbie, overcome by a sudden unexpected wave of sadness, was exactly what it was.

Chapter 2

Robbie crossed the grass and pressed the entry buzzer. After a few moments, he saw a bearded face at the tiny window, jaws busily working. Robbie had never seen Joe without a piece of gum in his mouth.

"Hi there, stranger!" Joe's voice held a strong hint of a mid-western drawl but Robbie had known him all his life. And knew that the closest Joe had ever been to cowboy country was a weekend trip to New York.

Joe stood and chewed, eyeing Robbie thoughtfully until he finally made up his mind. "Okay," he said. "You don't look very dangerous to me. Come on in."

"Hi." Robbie stepped gratefully inside, knowing Joe was bending, if not breaking, the rules. Only members of the research staff were allowed in the animal house. He smiled and reached up a hand to wipe his sweaty forehead, wondering why he felt so wobbly all of a sudden.

"Thought you were going away this weekend," said Joe, leading the way across the reception area towards an inner door.

"We were supposed to go to the cottage." Robbie made no effort to keep the resentment out of his voice. "But Dad said he had to work today."

"That's a pity." Joe slid a swipe card out of his shirt pocket and unlocked the door. "Don't think I'd fancy it myself, though. Must get pretty cold up there at this time of year."

"It does," said Robbie, just to be polite. He didn't care how cold it was. He loved going to the cottage. Last winter, they had arrived to find that the snow plough had only cleared the main roads. His dad had refused to risk the car on the potholed track up to the cottage and had tried to persuade Robbie that they might as well give up. But Robbie had eventually convinced him that they could walk the rest of the way and carry what they needed on their backs.

Robbie treasured the memory of the long trudge through the woods with nothing to break the stillness of the air except the creak of snow-laden branches, the crunch of their footsteps and the sound of their own laboured breathing. And most satisfying of all, that warm sense of coming home, when they finally emerged from the dim green tunnel to see the paint-blistered front door and the deep-set windows of the little house.

Joe tucked the swipe card into his shirt pocket. "I was sure your dad would sell that place when your grandmother died."

Joe was right. His father often talked about selling it. But he could do nothing until Robbie was old enough to agree. And Robbie knew he would never do that. He loved the place too much.

"He can't," said Robbie. "Grannie left it to me. It's *mine!"*

Joe chewed his gum a little harder and Robbie bit his lip, knowing he sounded like a spoiled brat. But his first sight of the huge room beyond the two locked doors drove the momentary embarrassment out of his head.

He had expected a bustling, crowded space filled with people. But the building was silent and empty. No one occupied the row of labs stretching all the way down one side of the building and, as far as he could see, there were no animals at all in the pens and cages that filled the open area in the middle.

"Where is everyone?" Robbie's voice sounded small and insignificant in the vast, echoing space.

"Get real, Robbie. You don't think I'd have let you in if there was anybody else around, do you?"

Robbie coughed. The stale, musty odour at the back of his throat was a strong reminder that this place had been home to a whole range of different creatures. He gestured at the empty cages. "But where are all the animals?"

Joe looked around, chewing fast again. "Used to be a lot busier than this," he agreed. "Especially when your mother was here. We made a good team, the three of us. But things got slower and slower after Jane died." He caught himself and looked down at Robbie with embarrassed sympathy. "Sorry."

"It's okay." Robbie knew all about his mother's trip to a conference in Bulgaria, when his unexpected early arrival had been followed by an infection the doctors could not control.

When he was younger, he used to believe he could remember a soft touch on his face, a whisper in his ear, even though he knew she died only a few days after he was born. Sometimes, he wished she was still here, but then at other times, he wasn't so sure. He already lived with one scientist. Perhaps two would have been twice as bad. He couldn't say that to Joe, though.

"Dad doesn't like to talk about Mum much."

Joe smiled at him. "I wish you could have known her, Robbie. Jane was a gifted scientist. She really loved her work." He was chewing fast again. Science was his favourite topic.

Robbie swallowed. It was hard to concentrate on what Joe was saying. His head was buzzing again and he looked around, hoping to find someplace where he could sit down. Joe didn't notice. He was in full flow.

"It's such an amazing feeling, to know you're reshaping the basic building blocks of life, making things that sometimes never existed before. And working with your mother was a real privilege. She was like an artist. Especially with the Hox genes. It took me years to duplicate her work ..."

He broke off and looked at Robbie curiously. "Are you okay? You look really pale."

"I'm fine." But Robbie wasn't fine at all. The insistent pull that had drawn him all the way from the car park to the animal house was fierce now, dragging him forward almost against his will. With a mingled sense of dread and expectation, he pointed to the far end of the building.

"What's down there?"

"Not much." Joe led the way. "We were involved in a project to reintroduce native species into the wild, natural predators, to keep the deer under control. But the focus has changed — now we're concentrating on specifics."

Robbie could tell Joe was quoting someone. From the buzzwords he had heard at home lately when his father was talking on the phone, it was almost certainly Gavin Moir.

In defiance of his growing nausea, he made a determined effort to look interested as he followed Joe down the central walkway towards the rear of the building. They stopped in front of a large cage set against the back wall.

Robbie peered through the wire, watching the animal inside pace restlessly from one side of the small space to the other. It was a cat, but much bigger than a wildcat, the only native Scottish cat he had ever heard of. He stared at its dark brown fur, dotted with lines of darker spots. "Is she a leopard?"

Joe's eyes shifted between Robbie and the cat. A puzzled frown creased his forehead. "How did you know she's female?"

Robbie frowned. He had been asking himself the same question. "Just a wild guess?"

"Well, you're right." Joe tapped gently on the roof of the cage. "Hello, Freya," he said softly.

The cat stopped pacing and moved closer to the mesh. Her whiskers twitched and Robbie saw the ruff of pale fur round her face fluff out like a hood. She was interested in the outdoor smell from his rain-dampened jacket. He looked at the tufted ears, the solid, muscular body and the oddly clubbed tail.

"Not a leopard." Joe confirmed what Robbie had already realized. "Although a lot of people think that, because of the spots. She's a lynx. From Norway. But cats like this used to live all over Europe, including Scotland."

"Why did you bring her here?" Robbie stared at the cat. The cat stared back. There was nothing there, nothing to explain the pressure that was now building up to the point where his head felt as though it might explode.

Joe bristled, feeling accused of something. "We didn't kidnap her, if that's what you mean. Freya got hit by a car. Her hip's pretty much healed now, though. Soon she'll be going back to where she came from. We took her because we were looking for another cat to keep this one company."

With a theatrical flourish, Joe waved an arm in the direction of a neighbouring cage. "Our very own Baldur, born two years ago, right here at the Institute." There was both pride and ownership in his voice.

Hardly able to think, let alone move, Robbie forced himself to turn and look. Shadows shifted at the back of the cage, unfolding into a creature of gold and black. The lynx stretched and yawned, then padded forward, looking up at him intently.

Robbie stared into those ancient, knowing eyes and felt a sudden jolt of recognition, even though he knew he had never seen this animal before. The tugging sensation intensified into a dizzying dislocation, as though his head had come adrift from the rest of his body.

He squeezed his eyes shut, opened them again and blinked, unable to make sense of what he saw. A series of squares floated in front of his eyes. It was mesh. Wire mesh. Beyond the wire he saw a face. There was someone was looking down at him — a boy with brown eyes, floppy dark hair and an expression of fixed disbelief. It was the face Robbie saw every morning when he looked in the bathroom mirror.

Chapter 3

Robbie tore his gaze away, breaking the contact. He staggered backwards, his heart pounding in his chest, his stomach heaving. The high-pitched yowl of an animal in distress set his teeth on edge, drowning out another noise, a repetitive burst of sound that his brain could not make sense of. It took him a moment to realize that the sounds were words. Someone was shouting at him.

"Robbie? Robbie! Are you all right?"

He put out a hand to steady himself and felt Joe take hold of his arm. Gratefully, he hung on, taking one wobbly step, then another.

"I'm fine," he managed, careful to keep his eyes away from the cage and the animal inside. "I just felt really dizzy for a minute."

With a tremendous effort, he steadied himself and let go of Joe's supporting hand. He was filled with a sudden urgent need to get away. The alien presence was still inside his head, nibbling at the edges of his mind, seeking a way back in. The atmosphere inside the animal house was now oppressively claustrophobic. He had to get outside.

"I'd better go," he said in a shaky voice. From the corner of his eye, he saw the gold and black shape flow to and fro across the front of the cage, its body pressed right up against the wire, as though trying to find a way through.

Joe looked at Robbie and then back at the cats. Robbie could tell that he knew something wasn't right. He just couldn't work out exactly what it was.

"I'd better go," Robbie repeated. "Dad will be wondering where I am."

"Are you sure you're all right?"

"I'm fine," Robbie insisted. "It's probably just something I ate."

The male cat — Baldur — had stopped moving. He sat with his face pressed up against the wire mesh, staring at Robbie, who pressed his hand against his forehead, fighting a powerful urge to look again at Baldur, knowing that the urge did not come from him. All he wanted was to get away from the cat as fast as he could.

"I'll walk over with you. You don't look very well to me." Joe was frowning, still glancing from Robbie to the cats, trying to work out exactly what had happened.

"No!" Robbie was desperate for some time on his own. "Please, Joe. Just let me out. I just need some air."

It took an immense effort of concentration to keep his legs steady until he reached the main door and stepped outside. He paused only long enough to make sure that Joe's face had disappeared from the window before he bent over with his hands on his knees, gulping in huge lungfuls of fresh air. The headache had disappeared and his stomach was slowly getting back to normal, but his mind still spun dizzily as he tried to make sense of things.

He had been looking at the female cat, Freya. That bit was clear. But then he had turned towards the other animal and something had twisted inside his head. It was as if the cat, Baldur, had hijacked his brain, forcing Robbie to look through the cat's eyes instead of his own. It was his face, but different from what he was used to. Duller. As though there wasn't enough colour in the world.

It wasn't possible. It couldn't be happening. His stomach lurched again and acid rose in his throat. He swallowed and leaned forward, afraid he was going to be sick, and stared down at the grass beneath his feet, concentrating on the tiny beads of rain glistening on each bright green stem. *This* was real; the grass, the rain, the cooling breath of wind against his flushed face. The rest was surely his imagination.

He glanced at the building behind him. Maybe he was going mad. Was it possible to be dreaming, even when you thought you were wide awake? Robbie had never heard of anything like that. He shook his head to clear his thoughts. He wasn't well, that was all. He just needed to go home.

He set off across the lawn, feeling a little better with every step he took. By the time he was climbing the broad steps into the main building, the strange feeling in his head had faded to the point where he could almost believe it wasn't there at all. But he had a deep suspicion that he was only fooling himself. It was like toothache, biding its time before erupting once again.

He hurried down the corridor, anxious to find his father, but before he even reached the door to Gavin Moir's office, he could hear raised voices coming from inside. He hesitated, knowing this was not a good moment to interrupt.

"I'm sorry, Michael." Moir's voice was hard and loud. "It's not your decision to make. This is fundamental research. We're putting this Institute — and this country — at the forefront of genetic research. I would have thought you'd be grateful that Joe has finally managed to move Jane's work forward. Believe me, it's going to attract great interest."

"Attract dollars, you mean!"

Robbie tensed. Dad almost never raised his voice, but he was shouting now.

He heard Moir sigh heavily. "I don't understand why you allowed this work to be abandoned."

"I told you why! Don't pretend you don't know!"

"We can't afford to underplay the value of the gene splicing that's been done here." That was Moir again. His voice took on a note of finality. "We've got a meeting with the funding committee in Edinburgh next Friday and I want you there with me. If that goes the way I hope, then — whether you like it or not — we *will* be introducing Baldur to the world."

There was a moment of silence. Robbie reached for the door handle. Then he froze, with one arm still outstretched. Moir's voice was quieter now, but Robbie had no trouble hearing what he said next.

"As for the rest, we can deal with that later. It's not in my interest — or yours — to let it become public knowledge. And there's no reason why it should. From what you've told me, the boy knows nothing."

Robbie heard his father speak through gritted teeth. "Robbie," he hissed. "The *boy* is called Robbie."

Very quietly, he let go of the door and retreated to a chair in the hallway, where his father found him a few minutes later.

Michael draped an arm round his Robbie's shoulder as they walked out the back door. Robbie looked up at him. His father was trying hard, but Robbie could feel the stiffness in his body and the note of strain in his voice after his argument with Moir.

"It's a bit late to get on the road now, don't you think? Maybe we should take in a football game instead. Or how about a swim?"

This came as no surprise to Robbie. He shrugged off his father's arm, refusing to answer.

"A swim then," said his father, clearly determined to ignore Robbie's lack of enthusiasm.

Nothing felt properly real for the rest of the afternoon. Robbie found it impossible to concentrate on anything. His thoughts jumped all over the place, trying to find some kind of reasonable explanation for what had happened in the animal house; that sensation of something trying to worm its way inside his head and then that sudden strange blip in reality when he thought he saw himself through Baldur's eyes.

And what about the argument between his father and Gavin Moir? Moir had mentioned Robbie's mother, something about the work she had been doing. But what did his mother's work have to do with him? And what was it that 'the boy' didn't know? From the sound of things, it was something both his father and Gavin Moir wanted to keep to themselves.

None of it made any sense. It was like trying to fit together a jigsaw puzzle without knowing what the whole picture looked like.

Eventually, Robbie gave up and flopped down in front of the TV. He needed answers. The trouble was he wasn't even sure what the question was. And he definitely didn't want to admit he had overheard that argument. Finally, he roused himself enough to put together a quick supper of beans on toast. When it was ready, he called his father from the study.

"Dad ..." he said tentatively, when they were sitting opposite one another at the kitchen table. "I went into the animal house today."

His father's head jerked up from his plate, his narrow face twisted in a ferocious frown. "You know you're not allowed in there!"

Shocked by the anger in his father's voice, Robbie faltered for a moment. But he was determined to carry on. "Joe said it was all right."

Michael said nothing, just bent back to his plate and carried on eating.

"Dad ... something weird happened."

His father's head came up again. "I've told you before, Robbie. Those animals are not pets. They are not there for your entertainment."

It was hard to continue with his father so determined not to listen, but Robbie ploughed on, determined to finish.

"I saw a cat ... a lynx ... and then ..."

Michael pushed his plate to one side and stood up. “I don’t want you anywhere near that place, do you hear me, Robbie?”

For once, his easy-going father was laying down the law. Robbie glared at him mutinously.

“But I need to tell you something! I need you to listen!”

Michael leaned across the table, his eyes hard and cold. He was gripping the edge of the table so hard his knuckles were white.

“It’s you who needs to listen, Robbie! And I’m telling you for the last time. Don’t let me catch you anywhere near the animal house.”

Without giving his son a chance to say another word, he slammed out of the kitchen and back into his study, leaving Robbie staring at his plate. Slowly and deliberately, he collected the cutlery and the dishes, then he turned and threw them against the wall.

Chapter 4

Robbie came downstairs the following morning to find his father already at the kitchen table, a cup of coffee in his hand.

"Do you want cereal? Or toast? There's some bread." Dad's voice was stiffly polite.

"Toast, please." Robbie's reply was equally cool.

He sat down and looked around. Apart from a few red smears on the kitchen wall and a sticky patch on the floor, all trace of last night's damage had been erased. The message was clear. As far as his father was concerned, last night's argument had never happened.

But it wasn't as easy as that for Robbie. Over the next few days, all through the daily business of home and school, his mind scurried first one way, then the other, like a rat in a maze. He wondered if maybe he should he go to the doctor. But how could he possibly describe what had happened? He couldn't even explain it to himself. And the doctor was bound to say it was all his imagination. But he hadn't imagined the argument. What was it the two men didn't want Robbie to know? And what did it have to do with Baldur?

In the end, he didn't bother with the doctor. There was no point. He felt perfectly well, except for the confusion of thoughts tumbling about inside his head. It was hard to keep his mind on what he was doing when the memory of what had happened to him in the animal house constantly intruded, like a torn fingernail snagged on a piece of cloth.

On Wednesday evening, he was at the kitchen table, staring down at his maths homework. Spike lay curled up on the table, his rumbling purr a comforting antidote to the blur of numbers and symbols on the page in front of him. Technically, the cat belonged to a family a few doors down the street, but he was always happy to keep Robbie company when his dad was out of the house.

Robbie sighed. His homework was already a day late. He would be in deep trouble if it wasn't handed in first thing tomorrow. But he couldn't seem to work it out, no matter how hard he tried.

Struck by a sudden thought, he reached out a hand and placed it on the cat's head. Spike and Baldur were both cats, but this one was far smaller and much less threatening that the lynx. He stroked the solid dome with his fingers, feeling the hard skull beneath the soft fur.

Cats were strange. It was as if they had two different personalities inside a single body. Indoors, Spike was about as threatening as a teddy bear. But outside, he was a ferocious hunter. He liked to bring Robbie presents — dead mice and birds, often still warm, sometimes with bits missing. It was one of the reasons Dad wouldn't let him in the house. Robbie often wondered what the cat thought of him when he scooped his gift on to the dustpan and dumped it in the rubbish bin.

Spike's leg twitched and he let out an odd little sound. Maybe he was dreaming of the hunt. Robbie felt his own body tense, imagining the final moments of that long, slow chase, muscles clenching, ready for that sudden final leap. And then the capture, teeth sinking into flesh and bone, releasing the hot, salty taste of blood ...

Robbie snatched his hand away. He stared at the cat. Had he really been thinking cat thoughts? Or was his imagination working overtime?

Spike opened one eye and looked at him, then closed it again. He was still purring. Robbie sighed again. He wasn't going to get anywhere with his homework. Especially without a pen. There was usually one lurking somewhere among the litter of papers on his father's desk.

He pushed back his chair and made for the study, where he flicked half-heartedly through the piles of paper on the desk, then rummaged about in the drawers. His eyes strayed towards the filing cabinet in the corner. Robbie had never thought much about it before. It was just part of the furniture. But he knew that was where his father kept all the stuff he had brought home from the Institute after his mother died. He couldn't help wondering if maybe the answers to some of his questions were in those drawers.

He moved across the room and tried one. It opened easily. They weren't locked. He hesitated for a moment, then reached in and pulled out a file, telling himself he had a right to know. Dad was wrong to shut him out. The file contained a copy of one of his mother's papers. He frowned down at the title. 'The Influence of Ancient Hox Genes on Mammalian Development.' Underneath was a brief summary of the work.

Robbie scanned it eagerly, hoping some useful fact might jump out at him. But he soon realized it was hopeless. It was like trying to read a foreign language. He could barely understand one word in ten. Defeated, he looked back at the title and murmured the words aloud, as though that might somehow make a difference.

He understood about genes. They made you what you were, a human or a cat. And mammalian must mean animals. Robbie frowned in concentration. The summary seemed to be about how Hox genes affected the way animals grew.

The only bit that made any real sense was the list of contributors. The first was Jane Bruce, his mother. Then came Joseph Barron. That was Joe. But there was another name on the paper. One he had never come across before. Stella Loomis. Robbie blinked. It was odd that no one had ever mentioned her. Joe had said there were three of them in the team, but Robbie had assumed the third person was his dad. And if her name was on the paper then she must have done a lot of the research.

He flipped through the rest of the file, but it was all the same incomprehensible jargon. At the back, he came across an official looking form, a request for leave on medical grounds. Robbie stared down at it. So his mother had got as far as booking time off to have her baby. But she never took that leave. The baby arrived too soon.

A scrap of paper fluttered to the ground. He bent to pick it up, but the sound of a car door slamming outside warned him he had run out of time. Hurriedly, he jammed everything back in the drawer, switched off the light and closed the door. By the time his father opened the kitchen door, Spike was outside, safe but disgruntled, and Robbie was back at the table, his homework spread out around him.

"I'm glad to see you didn't wait to be told," his father said dryly. He opened the freezer and removed a couple of ready meals. "Makes me think you must be up to something."

"Why would I be up to something?" Robbie hoped he didn't sound too defensive. "I just wanted to get it over with. There's something I want to watch on TV."

"Fair enough." Michael switched on the oven while Robbie stared down at a blank page.

"Are you stuck? Do you want some help?"

"No," said Robbie quickly. He didn't want his father to see the scribbled mess he had produced so far. "I just need a pen."

Hid dad stuck the food in the oven without bothering to wait for it to heat up. "There's probably one on the desk somewhere."

It was bedtime before Robbie rediscovered the note, crumpled up inside his trouser pocket. He must have stuffed it there instead of replacing it along with everything else.

He sat down on the bed and smoothed it out between his fingers. It was a list of jobs that the writer wanted someone to do. It finished off by saying the writer would come in to finish them off after the baby was born. But the signature at the bottom wasn't Jane Bruce. It was Stella Loomis.

He looked up as the bedroom door opened and his father poked his head inside.

"Are you off to bed? Good night then."

Robbie hesitated, remembering the furious reaction last time he asked his father a question. But he wanted to know. "Dad? Who was Stella Loomis?"

His father's face went from white to red and back to white again. His body stiff with anger, he advanced into the room, towering over Robbie.

"Where did you get that name?" He saw the piece of paper and snatched it from Robbie's hand. "I'm giving you one final warning, Robbie. Don't let me catch you poking your nose into things that don't concern you!"

"Don't they?" Robbie was red-faced now as well. A familiar feeling of frustration welled up inside Robbie. There had always been things his father refused to talk about. "What about Mum, then? Is she something that doesn't concern me?"

Michael's eyes narrowed. "What does your mother have to do with this?"

But Robbie turned away, refusing to answer. After a moment, he heard his father walk away. He jumped to his feet and slammed the door, then slumped back on the bed, all kinds of wild ideas flashing into his head. Maybe he was adopted. Maybe his mother was still alive. But then he checked himself. That was stupid. If Stella Loomis had a baby and gave it away, then Jane Bruce wasn't his mother at all.

He clenched his fists. None of this made sense. Of course he wasn't adopted. He dimly remembered Grannie, his mother's mother, telling him all kinds of stories. She would never have done that if Robbie wasn't really her grandson. She had even taken him to the cemetery, to visit his mother's grave.

Robbie threw his clothes on the floor and climbed into bed. Only a few days ago, life had been simple, even a little boring. It wasn't boring now. It was complicated and confusing. He punched the pillow hard and thumped his head down on top of it. There was so much he didn't understand. And his father would tell him nothing.

Sleep was a long time coming. Out in the street the noise of passing traffic gradually diminished into silence. A long time later, he heard his father in the bathroom, then the sound of his bedroom door closing. When he did finally fall asleep, it felt like only moments before he jerked awake to the sound of a motorbike roaring past the house. He lay in a tangle of covers, the sweat chilling on his body, waiting for the dawn. Somehow, in the night, a thought had come to him. There was one other person he could ask. He had to talk to Joe.

Chapter 5

Daylight sent some of Robbie's darker thoughts scurrying back into the shadows where they belonged. It wasn't so very strange that two women who worked together should both have had babies at the same time. What *was* odd was his father's angry reaction every time Robbie mentioned anything to do with his mother's work.

He eyed him thoughtfully across the breakfast table. Maybe Dad was the one who needed to see a doctor. But that was a scary thought. Firmly, he pushed it away.

"I'll be late again tonight, Robbie," Michael said as they left the house. "I've got a meeting to prepare for."

"Fine," said Robbie. "I'll go to Ally's." If this was the meeting Gavin Moir had talked about, then presumably Dad wouldn't be at work tomorrow. Not if he was in Edinburgh.

After his restless night, Robbie's brain felt as though it was wrapped in cotton wool. He sleepwalked all through school, unable to concentrate on anything for more than a couple of minutes at a time. His maths teacher opened his book and frowned down at it when Robbie handed it in, but he didn't care. If things worked out the way he hoped, then he wouldn't be here when it was handed back.

When the bell finally signalled the end of lessons he hurried out of the classroom, looking for Ally and the bus to Duncraig. The two boys had very little in common, apart from the fact that neither belonged to any particular crowd, but Ally was the closest thing Robbie had to a friend. Except for Spike.

Heading upstairs after tea, Robbie listened with only half an ear while Ally blethered on about the game level he had achieved the night before. Ally was eager to play, but the second time Robbie's character was very thoroughly killed, he lost patience and glared at Robbie in disgust.

"You're just not trying, are you? I might as well be playing with my little sister."

"Sorry." Robbie dropped the controls. "I've got other things to think about."

"Like what?" Ally demanded.

For a brief moment, Robbie considered telling Ally everything. It would be such a relief to have someone else to talk to. But it was too risky. Duncraig was a small place. If he mentioned the argument between his father and Gavin Moir, Ally might tell his mother and very soon, everyone would know that Michael Bruce had trouble at work. If Dad found out, he would know it could only have come from Robbie. But the argument was his only proof that whatever was going on at the lab had something to do with him. Without it he couldn't persuade Ally that his experience with the cat was more than just a weird mental blip.

He shrugged. "I've been trying to find out what kind of work my mother did."

"Well why don't you ask your dad then?"

Ally was right. It was the obvious solution.

He clamped down on the surge of resentment at the thought of his father.

"I don't want to upset him," he said, feeling slightly uncomfortable with the lie. "He doesn't like to talk about her."

Robbie felt a pang of guilt when he saw Ally flush with embarrassment. But he had no choice. It wasn't his fault that his father thought he was too young, or too stupid, to be trusted.

"You could try the internet," Ally offered.

"No thanks." It would just be more of the stuff he couldn't read yesterday. He needed someone who could explain. It had to be Joe. If he could get him on his own.

But that wasn't quite true. Robbie tilted his head thoughtfully. He couldn't use the computer at home in case Dad found out what he was up to. And he wasn't even sure if he'd know how to go about it anyway. But Ally would. He had a reputation as a bit of a computer geek.

"I've changed my mind," Robbie said. "Can we try now?"

Ally sighed, but he could hardly refuse to follow his own suggestion. "And then can we play after?"

Robbie nodded and Ally stood up. "Come on, then."

He pulled out a chair and sat down at his desk, with Robbie watching over his shoulder as the screen came to life.

"Can you look for Stella Loomis?"

Ally frowned up at him. "Who's she? I thought you were looking for your mother."

"She used to know my mum," said Robbie. "They worked together. I thought maybe if I knew where she was, I could talk to her instead of my Dad."

"Fair enough." Ally typed in the name, pressed enter and watched the results come up. He scrolled down the page, selecting one at random. "There," he pointed to an address at the bottom of the page. Stella Loomis worked at The Callander Foundation.

"Pretty good," said Robbie.

"It wasn't exactly difficult." Ally leaned back in his chair.

"There's no address, though."

"No problem." Ally entered another query in the search box. After only a couple of false starts, he found the Foundation website, then the contact details. "There you are," he said triumphantly. "It's in Callander. That's near the wildlife park. Remember we went there last year?"

"I remember," said Robbie. Dad had signed the permission slip before he found out where they were going. He had been annoyed when Robbie came home filled with excitement at the chance to see wild animals out in the open. But in the end, it had been a disappointment. The enclosures had been far smaller than he expected. As far as Robbie was concerned, the wire fences made it feel like a bigger version of a zoo.

Robbie stared at the screen, thinking hard. Callander was on the main road north. It couldn't be more than an hour away on the bus. If Joe did know what his father refused to tell him, then he had kept quiet about it for years. It might not be easy to persuade him to talk. And did he really want to risk another encounter with that creature in the animal house?

But then reality kicked in. He frowned and chewed thoughtfully on his lower lip.

"What's the problem?" Ally sat up, clearly disappointed at Robbie's unenthusiastic reaction.

"It doesn't really help much," said Robbie. "I can't just walk up to the security guard and ask him to let me in."

Ally leaned forward again. "Then maybe we can find out where she lives — it's not a very ordinary name."

"Can you do that?"

"Online white pages, stupid!" said Ally. "Don't you pay any attention in computing studies?"

"No," said Robbie. "I don't."

A few quick keystrokes and Ally had a phone number, and an address to go with it. Unable to resist showing off, he found another website and brought up a map, with a handy little arrow pointing directly at the house.

"Wow!" Robbie was genuinely impressed. "Can you print that out?"

"Okay," said Ally. "And then can we get on with the game?"

"If you like."

This time Robbie did his best to pay attention. He knew Ally deserved it. But it was getting harder and harder to concentrate. By the time his father arrived, his sleepless night had finally caught up with him and he lurched through the rest of the evening like a zombie, falling into bed far earlier than usual.

The next morning, Robbie watched his father stuff his laptop into his briefcase and then take an anxious look around, clearly wondering what he might have left behind this time.

"I shouldn't be too late — except they might want us to go for dinner afterwards."

"Don't worry." Robbie wanted his father out of the house as soon as possible. He lifted his own bag and headed down the hall. "Take as long as you like. I'll see you at Ally's house."

"Robbie, stop!"

Robbie halted, waiting while his father walked down the hall and laid a hand on his shoulder. Unwillingly, he turned to face him. He should have known it wouldn't be this easy. Dad must have noticed something wasn't right.

But his father asked no searching questions. Instead, he looked down at his son and said quietly, "I know this has been a bad week."

Robbie nodded, but he wasn't finished.

"I do know what I'm doing." Michael looked searchingly into Robbie's face. "It's all for the best, even if it doesn't look like it to you. I need you to trust me."

Robbie looked up into the thin, anxious face. He had no doubt that his father thought he was doing the right thing. But that wasn't good enough.

"Why should I trust you, if you won't trust me?"

"Well," said his father awkwardly, removing his hand. "I just wanted to explain things a little."

"You haven't explained anything, Dad."

Robbie hefted his bag on to his shoulder, opened the front door and set off towards the bus stop. But he didn't go beyond the first corner. Instead, he waited until he was sure his father was gone, then retraced his steps and slipped back inside the house to change out of his uniform. He had never skipped school before, but after yesterday's performance, they would probably just assume he was sick and that Dad had forgotten to let them know. After all, Robbie told himself, it wouldn't be the first time.

Chapter 6

All the way to the Institute, Robbie's shoulders itched. His school uniform was in his bag just in case he needed it later, but he still felt as though he had a sign on his back saying 'This boy should be in school.' Robbie knew there were people in his class who did this regularly and he wondered how they managed to be so casual about it. But then, they weren't usually on their own. And they weren't hanging around someplace as small as Duncraig.

He began to breathe more easily when he left the houses behind and turned down the small side road leading to the Institute. But even before he caught sight of its high roof poking up above a stand of trees, he could feel the first stirrings of that tug inside his head. Something — no, some-one — was trying to push their way in.

This time, though, Robbie wasn't going to be taken by surprise. He pushed back firmly and felt the sensation retreat, like a wave drawing back from the shore. There was no nausea, no dizziness. He smiled. It was going to be all right. He was in control.

His smile disappeared as soon as he approached the booth beside the main gate and saw a puzzled frown appear on the face of the man inside. It hadn't occurred to him how odd it might look, arriving alone and on foot.

"Hi, Robbie." The man put down his newspaper and leaned forward. "What are you doing here?"

"Hi, George," Robbie made an effort to sound casual. "I've come to meet my dad."

Robbie's heart sank when he saw George swivel round in his chair to check a board above his head. He hadn't realized there was a record of who went in and out.

George turned back to Robbie, his frown deepening. "Sorry Robbie, your dad's not here. He didn't come in this morning. Are you sure he told you to meet him here?"

Robbie thought quickly. "I know he's not. I talked to him on the phone. The heating broke down at school and they had to send everyone home. It was a bit of an emergency — he said I was to come here and wait in Morag's office until he picked me up."

George's gaze travelled doubtfully down Robbie's sweatshirt and jeans. Maybe it hadn't been such smart idea to change out of his uniform after all. But there wasn't much he could do about that now. He forced himself to stand still and plastered a look of confident expectation across his face.

At last George gave a slow nod. "All right then. In you go. I'll let her know you're on your way."

"I promised to see Joe first," Robbie said hastily. "We're organizing something. A surprise for Dad."

Fortunately, George wasn't too interested in Robbie's arrangements with Joe. He turned back to the board, made a note of his arrival and reached for the phone. "I'll tell her you'll be in her office in about five minutes, then."

Robbie set off for the animal house, deeply disappointed. Five minutes wasn't going to be anything like enough. But he had invested too much effort in creating this opportunity. He wasn't going to give it up now. And anyway, he could hardly tell George he had changed his mind.

"I need to talk to you," Robbie said as soon as Joe opened the door.

Joe leaned against the door. He cracked a chewing gum bubble between his teeth and looked thoughtfully down at Robbie. It didn't look as though he intended to invite him in.

"I wanted to talk to you about my mother. And Stella Loomis," he added, hoping the extra name might make some kind of difference.

Joe's face went still as stone. "Who told you?"

"Dad did." Robbie had no idea what they were talking about, but he wasn't going to let Joe know that.

"Michael? But he said no one ..." Joe pressed his lips together, then, slowly, he stepped aside. "If your dad told you, then I suppose that's his business. You'd better come in."

He led Robbie through the double doors into one of the glass-walled rooms running down one side of the building. As soon as Robbie stepped inside, he could feel the sudden interest of that watchful presence. It knew he was here. But this time Robbie was determined not to be taken by surprise.

Joe swung his legs over the chair beside the desk, and waved Robbie into another, watching him with a wary suspicion very different from his usual amiable expression.

Robbie glanced away, uncomfortable with Joe's intense scrutiny. The room was nothing special, the usual mix of well-worn equipment and shiny, high-tech modernity, like every other lab he had ever seen. The rest of the building was empty, just like before. It was an awful lot of space for two animals.

"Why is there nobody else here?"

"We've been winding things down," said Joe. "Getting ready. We're going to need every inch of this facility soon. People will be fighting to get lab space in here."

Robbie swallowed nervously, unsure where to start. It was hard to work out what to say and still keep his mind alert to that other presence.

He took a stab in the dark. "I know about the Hox genes."

"Of course you do," said Joe casually. "I told you about them last time you were here."

"Baldur has the Hox genes, doesn't he?" it wasn't hard to work out. Joe had said he was trying to repeat his mother's work. Robbie felt a surge of interest inside his head. Joe sat bolt upright in his chair and Robbie was suddenly sure that he was on the right track.

"Did Michael tell you that as well?"

Robbie nodded, struggling to keep a lid on his excitement. Right now he didn't care what lies he told, not if it got him closer to the truth. But it was probably safer just to keep his mouth shut.

Joe frowned. "Jane made a mistake — a big mistake." He held up a hand as though Robbie had been about to argue with him. "I don't really blame her, given the situation she was in."

Robbie was puzzled by the odd, pleading note in Joe's voice.

"I made a promise to your father, Robbie. I kept Jane's secret. I told nobody." He shrugged. "It didn't matter much anyway. I was getting nowhere. But then Gavin arrived, and we began to talk. He'd read every one of the Jane's papers and was determined that we would reproduce her work."

Joe seemed to have forgotten who he was talking to. He stood up and began pacing the floor. He snatched a piece of gum from the desk, unwrapped it and popped it in his mouth. "I know Michael wanted me to give it up, but he was wrong. Baldur is worth it — he's what we've been aiming for since the work began. And eventually someone was going to follow up our work. It's better that we do it here." Joe's eyes shifted to Robbie. "That way, we can keep a lid on everything else."

Robbie squirmed in his seat, uncomfortably aware that by now Morag would be wondering what was taking him so long. She might phone at any moment. And he still had nothing more than vague hints that something unusual, possibly dangerous, had happened in his mother's lab at about the time he was born.

"What happened to Stella Loomis and her baby?" Nervousness made Robbie clumsy. He blurted out the question.

Joe stopped pacing. Robbie wanted to kick himself when he saw surprise and then relief blossom on the man's face. Somehow he had got it wrong. He clenched his teeth in frustration. It was like playing a game without knowing the rules.

"You said mum made a mistake?" But he knew it was too late.

"Ah well ... we all make mistakes some time, don't we?"

Robbie could almost see Joe thinking, trying to remember what he had said and working out what to say next.

He watched Joe sit back down and plaster a smile on his face. "Your dad's been telling you about the work your mother did, is that it? And you wanted to know more?"'

Robbie nodded, wishing he had never opened his mouth in the first place.

"Well, I can tell you this much." Joe's smile widened. "When Gavin goes public with Baldur, Jane will get the recognition she deserves."

And so will you, thought Robbie. He hadn't missed the gleam of satisfaction in Joe's eye.

"So Baldur is part of the work she started?" he said carefully.

Joe nodded. "We're using the fertilization technique that Jane developed. Baldur is the closest we can get to the lynx that was native to Scotland thousands of years ago."

"But why did it take so long? It's been twelve years since mum died."

"There were ... issues," said Joe evasively. "Technical issues." He was getting uncomfortable again.

Robbie was determined to hang on. If he could just keep Joe talking, he might eventually get some clue about what it was he was so anxious to keep to himself.

"Is Baldur still part of the native species project, then?"

Joe shook his head. "Not really. Not any more. The female is going back to Norway. But not Baldur. Even if we wanted to, we wouldn't let him loose. He's too valuable — and nobody wants a genetically modified animal mingling with the wild population."

It was a struggle for Robbie to keep this conversation going and it wasn't made any easier by the uncomfortable realization that the presence inside his head was growing restless. "So what will happen to Baldur, then?"

Joe shrugged. "He stays here."

Robbie blinked. How could Joe be so calm about it? He was condemning a living creature to a lifetime inside a cage. Never to feel the earth beneath his feet, or the moorland wind in his face. Never to breathe the rich damp smell of the woods on a crisp autumn day. Always trapped. Always a prisoner, until the day he died.

The wail of grief and misery from the far end of the animal house warned Robbie that letting those thoughts loose inside his head was a serious mistake. The noise rose to an ear-splitting crescendo, drowning out the sudden, strident ringing of the phone, and then came the repetitive thud of a heavy body throwing itself over and over again at the metal walls.

Robbie clamped his head between his hands, as if that might somehow hold back the swelling tide of fear and desperation that soon obliterated every other thought.

Chapter 7

Joe jumped to his feet. Robbie's eyes jerked in his direction, but this time it was the other way round. This time, the cat saw what Robbie saw.

"Listen to that!" Joe peered through the glass partition, then turned to Robbie. "Wait here a minute, will you? I'll have to get something to calm him down."

Robbie saw Joe disappear through the door, then his eyes were dragged back to the desk, and the swipe card lying beside a half-empty coffee cup.

Not alone! Not alone again!

Robbie's brain whirled. This was far beyond feelings ... those were words, real words. How could a cat use human words? But he had no time to think about it. Grimly, he forced himself to fight back, struggling with fierce desperation to drive that persistent presence out of his head. At last he felt the pressure ease and eagerly pursued his advantage until his body was once more under his own control.

The relief was tremendous. But that other mind still called out to him in wave after wave of misery and fear. Wisps of someone else's memories floated through Robbie's head — the mewling cry of a seagull from the unseen world beyond the cold, hard cage. The scent of rain and grass, carried in on the clothes of the one who kept the keys.

It was too much. The pain was unendurable. Robbie knew if he didn't stop it, he would lose control again. And this time, perhaps, he would not be able to drive it back. He had to do something. He came close to panic when the thought brought a spurt of eagerness from the cat. He forced it away, trying to think calmly in spite of the insistent feelings of hope and anticipation that nibbled at the edges of his mind.

He grabbed the swipe card off the desk and jumped to his feet. Legs trembling, he made for the door, snatching a bunch of keys from a pin board on the wall as he passed by. The repetitive thudding from the cage stopped and he felt a surge of hope and joy that almost overwhelmed him.

Robbie hurried down the side wall and then over towards the cages, taking a route he hoped would keep him out of sight of Joe for as long as possible. He hadn't noticed that the phone had stopped ringing until he heard it begin again. Hands trembling, he sorted through the keys, careful not to look at Baldur in case he was sucked into those eyes again.

That one!

His fingers were slippery with sweat and it took several attempts before he got the key into the padlock and opened the door.

"That's it," whispered Robbie. He was shaking with tension, afraid to think what would happen when Joe discovered what he had done. "You can go now."

A whiskery face slid past his fingers and Robbie snatched his hand away. But Baldur only went as far as the next cage. He butted against the wire mesh with his forehead and Robbie saw Freya move forward, pressing against the cage until her nose touched Baldur's.

"Go *on,*" hissed Robbie. He could see Joe moving about in one of the side rooms, pulling open one cupboard door after another. It wouldn't take him much longer to find what he needed.

He looked down at Baldur. "Not her," he muttered. "Just you."

Baldur growled softly. He put one massive paw up against the cage. Robbie bit back a groan of frustration. He had done what he thought the cat wanted, but it was not enough.

Inside the cage, Freya began to prowl to and fro, stopping each time she reached the spot where Baldur's head rested against the mesh and rubbing her face against it. But Robbie couldn't — wouldn't — do what Baldur wanted. Freya was not raised with humans. She was a wild creature. And she was powerful; an animal built for strength and endurance rather than speed. Robbie shuddered at the thought of the damage she could inflict with that muscular body, sharp claws and razor teeth.

He knew that any minute now, Joe would find him with the keys in his hand and Baldur roaming free. Hardly able to believe what he was doing, Robbie unlocked the other cage and set off up the central aisle, both cats padding noiselessly behind him.

"Robbie!"

He froze. This was it. He was now in so much trouble it didn't bear thinking about. He looked round at Joe. A heavy body bumped against the back of his knees, urging him forward.

"Just give me a couple of minutes, will you?" called Joe. "Then I'll let you out."

Robbie stared stupidly for a moment before he understood. The cages lining the walkway hid his lower body — and they hid the cats as well. Joe thought he was on his own.

Robbie nodded in Joe's direction, not trusting himself to speak. It took all his self-control to resist the continuing pressure inside his head, demanding that he move forward.

Now, urged the voice. *Out. Now.*

A moment later, with a glance behind to make sure that Joe wasn't watching, Robbie was through into the outer hall and at the front door. He pulled the swipe card down through the lock and took a deep breath as he saw the green light wink. Then, with trembling hands, he pulled the door open and stepped outside.

Freya and Baldur slipped past him, whiskers twitching as they took in the outside world. Freya lifted her head to sniff appreciatively at the air, but Baldur's rising tide of excitement lasted only seconds before it shattered into a whirling disorder of birds and bushes, wind, sky and grass.

The cat's fear and confusion rose up to swamp him and Robbie took off, round the side of the animal house away from the main building, fighting his way mindlessly through the trees and bushes towards the boundary fence.

There was no time to worry about the fact that the cats kept pace with him. He raced for a spot where the bushes seemed thinner and dived towards the foot of the fence, clawing at the soil with his fingers. This was how he had found his way into the grounds on that long ago night when, as a young child, he had come in search of his father.

He forced himself into the hole, struggling to squeeze his body under the fence, twisting first one way, then the other. But he hadn't counted on the fact that he was no longer a small child. The hole was too small. His backpack snagged on the chain link fence and he was stuck, unable to move forward or back.

The impact of two heavy bodies hitting the wire shook the pack free. He coughed and spat, trying to clear the dirt clogging his nose and mouth and then, with a final, panic-fuelled struggle, he scrambled underneath the fence and out the other side. He looked up just in time to see Freya leap from the top in a graceful dive. A moment later, Baldur hit the ground beside him, landing in an awkward, clumsy tumble.

Galvanized by the sudden harsh scream of an alarm bell, he leaped to his feet. Joe would be organizing people to search the grounds, maybe phoning Gavin Moir. And Moir was with his Dad.

But Robbie had no time to think about it. He burst from the bushes on to the driveway, the cats still running with him, gravel spurting from beneath his feet all the way down the drive towards the road. Freya stopped and gave a deep-throated growl, staring intently at the tarmac surface while Robbie sped across to the other side and over a low stone wall into a field of stubble. But Baldur knew nothing of roads. He bounded across in pursuit of Robbie. After a moment's hesitation, Freya followed his lead.

The alarm shut off with a suddenness that made Robbie jump. His chest heaving, he gulped air into his tortured lungs. The two cats stopped beside him, both panting from the unaccustomed exercise. Baldur looked up at him expectantly, but Freya moved away, twitching her tufted ears as though trying to shake something free. She began to growl softly, and Robbie quickly grasped her meaning. She was not comfortable being so close to him. It wasn't surprising. Freya had known nothing from humans but pain and fear.

He knew he should never have let them out. At least the animal house was safe. And not just for Freya and Baldur. Robbie shrank from the thought of what might happen if someone passed by, out with a dog, or simply taking a walk. There was no space for animals like these in the human world. He had done something that was not simply stupid. It was dangerous. They had to go back.

But he barely had a chance to formulate the thought before a surge of rage and desperation threatened to engulf him. Baldur was free at last. He was not going back. And he was not going anywhere without Robbie, his one anchor in this terrifying new world.

Robbie felt the burden of responsibility settle on him like a dark, heavy cloak. He couldn't stay here. The first car along the road would send Freya into a panic. He looked beyond the fields, at the great, bare expanse of Sherrifmuir, its purple heather tinged with brown now that winter was on its way.

Ignoring the ache in his legs, he started to run again.

Chapter 8

Robbie crossed one field, then another. There was still no sign of pursuit. Deeply puzzled, he stopped and looked back.

A black shape swooped low with a raucous cry. Baldur flinched and Robbie felt a thread of panic slide into his head. Quickly, he sent a message back — a seagull's cry floating through an open window. Baldur looked at the crow, now winging its way towards a stand of trees, then turned to look at Robbie.

Robbie ignored him. He slid over the field wall, on to a narrow dirt track. From here, only a low fence separated the path from the wide expanse of the moor. He saw Freya bound past him, eager to reach the open countryside. Robbie followed more slowly, Baldur still close beside him.

They caught up with Freya easily enough. She was standing absolutely still, all her attention fixed on a white dot cropping the grass in the distance. Robbie watched the white dot moved slowly to another patch of grass. Perfect, he thought. A soon-to-be-dead sheep.

He set off again, angling away from the sheep, towards one of the rocky outcrops that studded the moor. Every so often, he stopped to look back, but there was still no one behind him. Just the cats, with Freya at the rear, plodding along in Baldur's wake. It seemed as though her need to be with Baldur was greater than her fear of human contact.

Robbie clambered up and sat down with his feet dangling above the heather. He could see a long way from here. If anyone came after them, he stood a faint chance of separating himself from the cats before they got here. He wished he was alone, away from the constant nag of someone else's thoughts inside his head, but his hope that the animals might wander off evaporated when he saw Baldur flop to the ground below him. Freya joined him a moment later, beginning what was clearly going to be an extensive grooming session.

Robbie sighed. How on earth had he got himself into this mess? He only meant to talk to Joe about his mother's work. And now here he was; a fugitive and a thief. Baldur didn't belong to him, and neither did Freya. They were the property of the Institute.

But then it hadn't been him making the decisions. Not really. He glanced down.

"It was you," he said softly.

Baldur looked up briefly, then went back to washing his shoulder with long sweeps of his rough tongue. Twice now, the cat had erupted into Robbie's head with a force he could not control. He had to make sure it didn't happen again. But how? He needed a barrier, something the cat could not cross. Robbie leaned back against the rock, imagining a wall inside his head, building it up, brick by brick. Baldur's ears twitched and Robbie felt sure the cat knew what he was doing.

As the morning wore on, Robbie stayed where he was, unable to think of anything else to do. The distant fields remained bare and empty but he had no doubt that eventually Institute security, or the police, would follow his path. He shrank from the thought of what would happen when they finally caught up with him. At the very least, he would be grounded for the rest of his life.

It wasn't fair. He had tried to explain, but Dad had refused to listen. None of this would have happened if he hadn't been forced to go and talk to Joe. Something about the research in the lab involved him, and the cat, too. Something his mother had done, something that Joe and his father were determined to keep quiet about. He shifted restlessly against the rock. It had all been a waste of time. He was in all this trouble for nothing.

He leaned over for his bag and rummaged inside. At least he had brought his packed lunch with him. The cats watched him avidly as he unwrapped the cling film from a cheese sandwich. After a moment, he tore the sandwich in two and tossed it down.

"You'd better make it last," he said, reaching for another one. "There's not much more."

Freya chomped up her piece in one quick bite, but Baldur was not so keen. He sniffed his portion, pushing it around with his nose, then he turned his head away. It didn't require any mind reading to get the message. Robbie watched Freya snatch up Baldur's share and claim it for her own. If the cat was going to be that fussy, then he wouldn't last long out here.

Freya lifted her head and sniffed the air, her ears erect. She looked around, first one way, then the other, before she stood up, clearly interested in exploring this new territory. Robbie thought he should maybe have let her chase that sheep. At least then the cats would have stayed near the farmland.

She took a few steps away from the rock and Robbie began to hope this might be his chance to separate himself from the cats, but Baldur only sighed heavily and curled himself into a tight ball with his head on his paws. It was obvious that the outside world was far more threatening than the cat had imagined. After a moment or two, Freya turned back and padded over to join him.

Eventually Robbie grew chilled from sitting on the bare rock. He stood up and began to pace along the top of the boulder, stamping his feet to get some warmth back. He could not understand why no one had come. And he knew he couldn't go back — Baldur wouldn't allow it.

He reached the end of the rock and peered into the distance. Callander was over there, behind the hills. Robbie had a knack for finding his way back to anyplace he had ever been. He had had no idea it was unusual until he had watched a film on TV one night about three pets travelling hundreds of miles to catch up with their family. Up until then, he had just thought everyone could do it.

Robbie had never been to the main part of Callander, but that wasn't much of a problem. He hadn't bothered to empty his bag before he flopped into bed last night and Ally's map was still inside. He looked thoughtfully at his feet, then back at the distant hills. His school boots were sturdy and his jacket was wind and waterproof. It would save a lot of time if he cut directly across the moor instead of following the road. And if he wanted to talk to Stella Loomis, he had to do it today. This would be his last free day for a long, long time.

He chewed his lip, trying to make up his mind. He could sit here, getting steadily colder until someone finally turned up, or he could walk. And if he was walking, there was a much better chance that eventually the cats would find something more interesting than he was and take off on their own. Making up his mind, he pulled on his pack and scrambled down from the rock. Baldur rose to his feet as soon as Robbie hit the ground. Freya followed a few moments later.

But Robbie's brisk walk turned almost immediately into a nightmare. Baldur was fearful and skittish, insisting on sticking to Robbie's side like a limpet. He bounced sideways whenever anything brushed against his fur, sending Robbie staggering off balance, and yowled in shock and distress when a hidden dip in the heather sent him stumbling into standing water.

Robbie soon grew frustrated at his slow progress, but there was no way to move any faster when the only way he could stop the cat's fear from overwhelming him was to send constant messages of explanation and reassurance. It was like helping a blind person to see.

A rising undercurrent of pain and discomfort told him that Baldur's tender paws were now raw and blistered, but even so, there was not the slightest indication that he intended to be left behind. And Robbie was having problems of his own. The twisted, knotty heather roots forced him into an awkward, high-stepping walk that strained his muscles to the limit.

Late in the afternoon, the sky darkened. Grey cloud gathered overhead and shortly afterwards a thin rain swept across the bleak landscape. Robbie watched the cloud descend. By the time it wrapped the moor in damp shreds of mist, he was ready to acknowledge that he had made the wrong choice. He should never have started walking so late in the day. And he was absolutely sure he didn't want to be out here when darkness came.

He turned round and faced Baldur. "This is no good. I'm going back."

From the way Baldur planted himself firmly on the ground in front of him, Robbie could tell that the cat understood perfectly.

He took a step forward, hoping Baldur would get out of the way. Instead, the cat's ears flattened against his skull and his lips curled in a ferocious snarl. Freya sat down nearby, watching with keen interest.

"You won't hurt me," Robbie said to Baldur. He took another step.

His eyes flicked across to Freya and he saw she was now lying full length on the ground, her back legs hunched, eyes fixed on him. A few seconds later she began to slither forward on her belly. With a jolt of terror, Robbie realized that she was stalking him. He watched her edge closer, all his instincts telling him to run, but he couldn't move. It was just as well. He knew that it would be a very bad mistake to turn his back on her. So he stayed where he was, rigid with fear afraid to move, afraid even to speak.

All right!

Baldur responded immediately to Robbie's unspoken message. He jumped to his feet and walked over to Freya. He nudged her, then licked her face until slowly the tension left her body and she began to relax. Robbie remained where he was until he was sure she had lost interest in him and then, defeated, he turned and walked on.

A little while later he stopped and stripped off his wet jeans. His school trousers were thin, but at least they were dry. He pulled them out of his bag and stepped into them, his teeth chattering as the wind danced around his bare legs. After a moment's thought, he put the wet jeans back on top. Two layers were probably better, even if one was wet. He pulled off his jacket, added his school sweatshirt to the one he already wore, then put the jacket back on top. It was the best he could do. Wearily, he set off again, bulkier but not a great deal warmer.

As the rain diminished and the last remnants of mist shredded away, the moor re-emerged, bathed in pale, watery sunshine. Robbie plodded on, anxiously scanning the bare expanse of grass and heather for anything that might offer a shelter for the night. The cats walked beside him, their fur dirty and bedraggled, their legs clumped with mud while slowly the sky darkened into night. At one point Robbie opened his bag and fished around to find that all the food was gone. He felt a brief flicker of hope when his fingers closed around his mobile, but that faded as soon as he looked at it. There was no signal.

No one was coming to get him. All he could do was to keep going.

As the land rose, the heather gave way to scrubby grass. It was easier walking, but by now Robbie's legs were trembling with exhaustion. The world narrowed to the way ahead and the two animals beside him. There was a tightness in his gut, and waves of discomfort from his empty stomach.

Finally, after one fall too many, he stopped in the lee of a stunted thorn tree, its twisted wind-blown branches bending over until they almost touched the ground.

"I need to rest. Just for a minute," he muttered, as if he needed to explain his decision to some invisible companion.

As the sky darkened into night, he settled himself as best he could, shifting about, hoping to find a comfortable position. He mustn't fall asleep, he reminded himself. If the weather turned treacherous, he might never wake up again. Tomorrow, he thought drowsily as he closed his eyes. Tomorrow he would see Stella Loomis and everything would be explained ...

In the end, it wasn't caution that kept him awake, but the constant pressure of another mind, struggling with its own burden of pain and exhaustion. Robbie slept only when Baldur slept, and Baldur hardly slept at all. He woke constantly, unable to make sense of this strange new world. The wind in the grass, the spatter of raindrops on the branches above them — even the scrape of Robbie's boots as he shifted position was enough to renew Baldur's deep fear of this dark, cold wasteland. But all the time, beneath all the pain and discomfort, Robbie sensed a deeper thread of joy. Baldur was frightened, he was hungry and every muscle in his body ached. But he was free.

Gradually, as the night wore on, cat and boy moved closer together. Robbie lay with Baldur's soft, warm body beside his, sensing how the cat took comfort from his presence. Despite everything, he found himself grateful for the warmth and the company.

At last, a faint gleam in the east signalled that dawn was not far off. As soon as it was light enough to see the way, Robbie pulled himself up and set off, footsore and weary to the bone. It was no surprise any more when the cats lurched to their feet and followed along behind him.

He stumbled to the top of a small rise and came to a stop. The empty moorland had stretched ahead of him for so long that at first he was unable to make sense of what he saw. He stared down at the fence that barred his way. Beyond it, barely visible in the grey dawn light, were all four lanes of the main road north.

Chapter 9

Trying to ignore the pain from his aching muscles, Robbie hauled himself over the fence. A wave of frustration from Baldur followed him as he slithered down the slope and came to a halt in the shelter of a prickly gorse bush. He didn't need to look back to know that Freya was probably still on the other side of the fence with her eyes fixed on the road.

A car hurtled past and Robbie watched its taillights disappear round the corner. He considered waving the next one down and asking for help. But the cats were clearly visible above him. A hysterical giggle rose in his throat at the thought of what a passing motorist might make of Robbie demanding a lift, accompanied by two huge cats.

But surely the road meant that he could now at least make a phone call. With renewed hope, he pulled out his mobile and turned it on. But there was nothing. He bit his lip in frustration, knowing that by now his dad must be frantic with worry. He looked across the road, where another grassy bank rose up to match the one he was sitting on. That was probably why the phone didn't work. If he could get over that hill, he was bound to pick up something.

But a phone call wouldn't be much use if he couldn't tell Dad where to find him. He pulled out Ally's map and frowned down at it, studying it as carefully as the dim light and his tired mind would allow. He could see the road, just inside the edge of the map. A little way beyond it a thin blue line marked the route of a river, running all the way into Callander. Thoughtfully, he let his grubby finger travel along the line. He had almost made it.

He heard the groan of metal and looked up to see Baldur leaning against the fence, his anxious eyes fixed on Robbie. Flashes of pain told Robbie that the cat's tender paws found the wire mesh hard to endure. He watched Baldur drop back to the ground and circle round behind Freya, nipping her, trying his best to herd her towards the barrier. But Robbie didn't think he'd have much luck. It didn't look as though Freya would ever cross that road.

Turning away, he dismissed the cats from his mind. What mattered now was persuading his tired legs to carry him over the road and up the hill on the other side. He stood up and stuffed the map and the phone in his pocket. At least he now had a rough idea of where he was. But already one car had flashed by while he was sitting there. Traffic would soon be building up. If he was going, it had to be now.

There was only one other thing he had to worry about. Bracing himself for the challenge he knew was bound to come, he slid down the rest of the slope and stepped forward, heading for the lay-by on the other side of the road.

No!

The message slammed into Robbie's head, backed by an almost overwhelming determination. But Robbie was determined too — he was going to cross this road and nothing that Baldur could do was going to stop him. He fought back with his own strength of purpose, feeling a warm glow of delight at the realization that if he concentrated hard enough, then he, too, could dominate the link.

But his triumph was short-lived. Behind him, the chain mesh rattled again and moments later, Baldur appeared at his side. The cat let out a distressed 'meep' and looked back at Freya while Robbie limped as fast as he could towards the central aisle, conscious that at any time, something might appear on the empty road. And at this time of the morning, it would probably be travelling too fast to stop.

He turned to see Baldur straddling the white line between the lanes. For once, he had his back to Robbie, watching Freya with a fierce intensity. She was over the fence now, scrabbling down the hill to the side of the road, her stubby tail jerking to and fro and her head going from side to side as though trying to dislodge some unpleasant memory. Suddenly, with a wail of pure terror, she plunged on to the road, catching up with Baldur and racing alongside of him as he chased after Robbie.

From the corner of his eye, Robbie noticed a Land Rover pull into the lay-by in front of him, but he had no time to worry about what its occupants might think of a boy and two huge cats appearing out of nowhere. He still had the rest of the road to cross.

He climbed over the central barrier and ran without stopping until he reached the safety of the other side, where he stopped and turned, gasping for breath, to see the two cats racing after him, their ears flat, eyes wide with terror, as a huge container lorry rushed towards them.

They made it only just in time. The lorry hurtled on, horn blaring, close enough that the wind of its passing knocked Robbie to the ground and sent the two cats leaping up the grassy bank in a frantic rush.

He had no time to recover before someone seized his arms in a crushing grip and dragged him to his feet.

"The boy! Do the boy first, then the cats!"

Robbie looked up into the unshaven face and angry eyes of Gavin Moir. He turned his head a fraction to see Joe standing a few steps away. His eyes widened in disbelief when he saw the rifle cradled in his arms.

"Hang on a minute!" Joe lowered the rifle. "I agreed to keep this quiet — I didn't agree to shoot a kid! I thought we were here to rescue him."

"Take him then!" Moir shoved Robbie into Joe's arms and grabbed the rifle. "Don't let him get away. I'll do the cats myself."

As Joe dragged Robbie across the gravel and bundled him into the back of the Land Rover, he saw both cats standing at the top of the bank, making two perfect silhouettes against the morning sky. Moir was struggling with the rifle, clearly unused to the weapon. But it wouldn't be long before he worked it out.

Robbie squirmed in Joe's grasp. "Let go! You're hurting me!"

"Listen to me, Robbie!" Joe gave him a hard shake. There was no trace now of any American drawl. His accent was pure Glasgow.

"You were going to shoot me!" Robbie couldn't even believe he was saying it. He twisted and pulled, but Joe's grip was like iron. He pushed Baldur's fear and confusion out of his head. He had no mental space left to cope with it. It was hard enough to deal with his own panic.

Joe merely held on tighter as Robbie struggled to free himself. "Stop it, Robbie! It's not what you think! It's a tranquillizer gun. It puts you to sleep."

"Let me go!"

"This is my fault." Joe frowned. "I should never have let you near the animal house. But I never thought this would happen." He stared down at Robbie. "You have to give this up. You're on your own. There's no one looking for you. No one to help you. Only us."

Robbie stopped struggling.

"That's better." Joe relaxed a little. "You don't understand, Robbie. Your dad won't go to the police. He knows how important it is that we keep this to ourselves. Believe me, you don't want to know what might happen if people start asking awkward questions."

He had no chance to say more before Robbie sank his teeth into his arm. Swearing, Joe snatched his hand away and Robbie took his chance. He burst from the Land Rover, running for the hill, and the cats.

Moir saw him coming and headed towards him, trying to cut him off. Robbie jerked sideways, eluding Moir's grasping hand and then dashed up and over the hill, plunging recklessly down, with the cats at his side. He tripped over a clump of grass, lost his balance and fell the rest of the way, rolling downhill until he crashed with a bone-jarring thump into a tumbledown wall.

He scrambled to his feet and looked up to see Moir at the top, struggling to get a clear sight with the rifle. Joe was already half way down, heading towards him with a grim look on his face, but he slithered abruptly to a halt when Freya turned to face him and let loose a deep, warning growl.

Joe stood very still. "Robbie, I want you to listen to me," he said carefully, all his attention fixed on the cat. Freya stared at him with her lips drawn back, showing the tips of her pointed teeth.

"This is silly," said Joe. "You have to come with us. We need to take you and the cats back where you belong."

Robbie glanced towards the wood on the other side of the wall, then looked back at Joe. He was tempted. If he did what Joe wanted, then in less than an hour, he would be home. And he was so very, very tired.

But Robbie didn't trust Joe any more — and he certainly didn't trust Moir. And not just because of the cats. He was beginning to wonder what they might have in mind for him, too. Robbie licked his dry, cracked lips, knowing he had to make up his mind. Baldur was waiting.

He couldn't understand it. Why didn't Baldur run? Why was the cat's need to be with him so much stronger than his fear of capture? The sense of grief that washed over him as Baldur contemplated a return to his prison was more than he could bear. He shook his head. It was no use. He couldn't do it.

"Run!" He reinforced the word with such a powerful mental shove that Baldur took off as if he really had been shot. Freya twitched her tufted ears at Joe, clearly making some kind of point, before she followed Baldur over the wall.

Joe made one last try. "Robbie," he pleaded. "You don't understand. These animals aren't pets. They're dangerous."

"Not as dangerous as you, Joe," Robbie said. "At least they've never tried to hurt me."

He looked up to see Moir glance uneasily at the road behind him. The traffic must be building up now. Moir lowered the rifle and gestured for Joe to join him.

"Leave it!" he yelled. "Look at them! They're not going to get much further. We'll pick them up later."

Robbie turned away, climbed shakily over the wall and set off into the wood.

Chapter 10

Robbie and the cats stumbled out of the trees to find themselves at the edge of an undulating series of fields, criss-crossed by a series of small roads. After the night on Sherrifmuir, it was strange to see farm buildings dotting the landscape, smoke spiralling up from their chimneys. Under those grey slate roofs, there were people waking up from a warm, comfortable night's sleep, looking forward to breakfast.

The panic-driven energy generated by his encounter with Joe and Gavin Moir soon drained away, but Robbie was anxious to put as much space between him and the road as he could. He forced one leaden foot in front of the other, until eventually his legs crumpled and he sank down in the shelter of an overgrown hedgerow. The cats dropped to the ground, tongues lolling, and closed their eyes.

Robbie lay on the soft grass, every muscle in his body burning, and gave himself up to exhaustion. But he still couldn't rest. Every time he closed his eyes, he saw Joe's face above him, hard and angry, his eyes like flint. After a while, he rolled over on one elbow and rummaged in his pocket for his phone. His heart lifted when he saw the bars light up at last.

He had a raft of messages, all from his father. The first one had arrived only a few minutes after he ran from the animal house. So Joe must have phoned Moir as soon as he discovered the cats were missing! Robbie frowned. It must have been Moir who told him to shut off the alarm. And now he knew why. It was obvious after that encounter on the motorway that Moir didn't want anyone to know that his prize specimen had disappeared.

And that was also why no one had come after them. But how did Moir know the cats were out on the moor, safely out of the way of people and houses and traffic? He and Joe must have been cruising the motorway, waiting for Robbie and the cats to appear. Somehow they knew exactly where and when they would leave the moor to cross the road.

Robbie was too tired to pursue it. He flicked through the rest of the messages. They started out confused and then angry, but it wasn't long before Robbie heard panic and then fear in his father's voice. Robbie swallowed a lump in his throat, overcome by a longing to talk to him. Dad would know what to do.

He answered on the second ring, his voice awash with relief. "Robbie! At last! Are you all right? Where are you?"

"I don't know," said Robbie hoarsely, fighting back the tears.

"I came back home as soon as I heard what happened," said his father. "I thought I'd better wait here in case you came back. But Gavin and Joe are out looking for you. Are you anywhere near a road? If you are, they can find you."

"They already did. Moir tried to shoot me."

His father sighed. "Don't be silly, Robbie. Of course he didn't."

"He did, Dad." Robbie's voice quavered. "What's going on? What is this is all about?"

"Robbie, there's nothing going on. I told you that already." His father's voice was stern now.

"But there is. I know there is," insisted Robbie. """I heard you talking to Gavin Moir. Something about me ... and Mum."

"That's nonsense, Robbie," snapped his father.

"If it's all nonsense, then why haven't you told the police?"

He heard a rush of indrawn breath, then, "I told you before. You just have to trust me." Michael's voice grew stern. "I want you to do as you're told. Find a road and wait for Joe and Gavin. Do you understand me?"

Robbie cut the connection and stared down at the phone. So not even his father was prepared to tell him the truth. And why was he so determined not to listen? But Robbie didn't really need to ask. He could answer that question for himself.

"It's because he's a grown up," he muttered resentfully, pocketing the phone. "And I'm just a kid."

He curled up beside the cats and closed his eyes. He would rest, just for a little while. And maybe then his tired brain would be able to work out what to do. It was his last conscious thought before his mind closed down.

A distant rumble penetrated his consciousness. He jerked awake and stumbled to his feet, thinking at first it was a roll of thunder. It took him a moment to work out where he was. He rubbed his eyes and looked around to see both cats lying side by side nearby. Baldur had his eyes on Robbie. Freya was watching a massive machine moving slowly across the field. It was the noise of the harvester that had dragged Robbie out of his exhausted sleep.

He ran his fingers through his matted hair, searching the hedgerow for a space wide enough to squeeze through. Still half asleep, he fought his way through the thorny branches into the next field, and then he stopped, unsure what to do next. He knew his father wanted him home. But Dad didn't understand about Joe and Gavin Moir. Probably because he didn't want to. His job meant everything to him.

A crackling of branches signalled the arrival of Freya and Baldur.

"I'm going to Callander," said Robbie. "And I suppose you two will be coming with me." He felt a little foolish talking out loud to two cats, but Baldur looked at him as if he could understand everything he said.

He knew now that he couldn't return the cats to the Institute. Maybe Stella Loomis would have more respect for Baldur and Freya than Joe did. He would take the cats to Callander and then he would go home and face his father. He didn't know if it was the right decision, but he couldn't think of anything else to do. He would have to be careful, though. After their conversation yesterday, Joe might work out that Robbie knew how to find Stella Loomis. And if he guessed where Robbie was going, then he would certainly tell Moir.

He looked down at the cats. They were clearly

just as hungry and exhausted as he was, their fur matted and their skin sagging in places that only yesterday had been densely packed muscle.

"I don't suppose I look much better," he said, making a half-hearted effort to pick twigs and straw from his hair and brush down his clothes before they set off.

It was one of those windless late autumn days when the skies are clear and it almost feels like summer. Robbie's body soon began to prickle with sweat. He took off his jacket and tied it round his middle, but he was stuck with the extra sweatshirt and trousers. In his rush to escape from the Land Rover, he had left his pack behind.

Avoiding open land, he kept to the hedgerows and woods, where the mottled fur of the lynx blended so well with the autumn reds, golds and browns that sometimes even Robbie couldn't tell exactly where they were.

They will find you. His father's words echoed in his head, leaving him with the uncomfortable knowledge that it would be a bad idea to stop for too long. Robbie's unease affected Baldur too. Every so often the cat stopped and turned, scanning the way they had come, his ears pricked forward to catch any suspicious noise. Baldur seemed to think they were being followed. But Robbie could tell the cat's senses were too confused by the innumerable signs and scents left by other people to be sure. In the end, he decided there was nothing he could do about it except to keep moving forward. His empty stomach ached with tension every time they crossed a road, but he saw no sign of the Land

Rover and began to allow himself to hope that the confusing network of small lanes meant that Moir could not easily tell where they were.

In the end it was the roads, not the open land, that gave the cats an opportunity to ease their hunger. Freya still growled every time she crossed a man-made surface, but her confidence was growing. Eventually she stopped and sniffed at a pathetic bundle of fur lying close to the verge, nosing it about until finally she gripped it in her jaws and carried it with her into the bushes. Robbie crossed the road behind her and sat down nearby, trying to ignore the sound of bones crunching between sharp teeth. And Baldur was eager to claim his share.

After that, both Freya and Baldur insisted on taking a few precious moments to forage up and down every road they crossed, while Robbie stood waiting in the undergrowth, rigid with tension. He didn't really want to look at what they were eating, but he couldn't help noticing. Rabbit mostly, and pheasants — even a squirrel, once. It was amazing — and a little shaming — to realize how many creatures ended up as "road kill."

They avoided the busier roads, but they still had one close call, when Freya decided to drag yet another small body into the bushes just as a car came round the corner. Robbie caught a brief glimpse of a youngish man in a business suit, his jaw dropping open in astonishment. The car wobbled alarmingly from one side of the road to the other before it disappeared round the bend.

"That's going to be one for the local paper," said Robbie. He looked thoughtfully at Freya.

"I bet that's what got you run over in the first place."

Freya didn't bother to look up. Her hunger satisfied, she left the remains for Baldur and began to clean her fur. Robbie lay back and closed his eyes, grateful for the chance to rest.

Something heavy pinned him to the ground and his eyes flew open to see Freya looming above him. He lay there, terrified, as he saw her jaws open to reveal razor sharp teeth. A tongue like sandpaper rasped across his face and over his head, leaving his skin tingling. Then she lifted her paw and began licking it clean while Robbie stared up at the sunlight dappling the leaves, waiting until his heart stopped pounding. It seemed that Freya had finally decided he was a friend.

Not long after, they stopped again, this time at a picnic area beside a tumbling river. While the cats moved eagerly towards the water, Robbie stopped beside the wooden table and looked upstream. This must be the river that flowed through Callander.

"Not far now," he muttered in satisfaction. "Not far now."

Robbie felt a surge of pleasure from Baldur and turned to see him standing in the middle of the river, the cool water washing over his tender paws. In spite of everything, he smiled to see how Baldur found joy in things that Robbie had taken for granted all of his life.

Robbie's eyes flickered across the table and locked on to the metal bin beside it. Someone had dumped the remains of a picnic. Once it caught his attention, Robbie found he was unable to look away. His stomach rumbled, demanding food, but his mind rebelled at the thought of eating someone else's leftovers.

Hot tears of shame sprang into his eyes as he walked slowly towards the bin. Angrily, he brushed them away and lifted out a carrier bag containing a half-eaten sausage roll, some crumbly pieces of cake and an unopened packet of crisps. After the first tentative bite, he wolfed down the rest and was surprised to discover that it tasted better than anything he had ever eaten before.

He stuffed the bag back in the bin, bent down to pull off his boots and socks, then hurried down to the water to join the cats.

Chapter 11

For the first time in over twenty-four hours, Robbie was back in the human world. He told himself there was nothing particularly unusual about a boy out walking on a Saturday afternoon, although he couldn't help but notice that most people gave him a wide berth as soon as they took in his bedraggled appearance.

His initial worries about the cats soon disappeared when he realized they were only interested in remaining unseen, melting into the underbrush at the first hint of a human presence. All the same, a lot of people out walking their dogs along the familiar path must have gone home puzzled — and probably a little concerned — when their pets were roused to savage barking and deep-throated growls as their keen noses scented something mysterious lurking in the bushes.

According to his map, Callander was at the foot of Ben Ledi, the first of the northern mountains, and Robbie realized the town couldn't be far away when he saw the land across the river begin to slope upwards. On this side, though, the path remained level as it meandered among the trees.

Gradually the houses he glimpsed beyond the trees grew smaller and more frequent. He began to hear the hum of constant traffic. It was late afternoon and the park across the water was still crowded with people enjoying the mild autumn weather. The woodland walk continued on, right through the town, offering plenty of cover for the cats. His side, too, was much busier now. He stepped to one side to avoid a family group with bikes and pushchairs, frowning a little as he sensed Baldur's growing unease. If Baldur was nervous, then surely Freya felt the same.

With mingled relief and apprehension, he saw a bridge leading across the river a little way ahead. The bridge was marked on the map. He was nearly there. As he walked past the bridge, he saw a small path running down from the street towards the river walk. The house that Robbie wanted was the one at the end of the row, next to the path.

His pace slowed. He took one step forward, then another, and finally stopped. He wasn't ready. He had no idea what he wanted to say. This was a woman he had never heard of until a few days ago. She seemed to have had no contact with the people she had once worked with. And what would she make of a grubby boy in crumpled clothes wanting to ask questions about the work she had once done with Jane Bruce? The river gurgled and chattered its way over the rocks, but nothing could drown out his thoughts. It was stupid, to think of turning up on this woman's doorstep trailing two dangerous animals along with him.

An enquiring mental nudge from Baldur reminded him that he didn't really have any other choice. And what difference did it make? Things were already as bad as they could be. Talking to Stella Loomis couldn't make them any worse. And he hadn't forgotten about Joe and Gavin Moir either. It wouldn't be a good idea to risk being seen on the street, but it looked as if the people who lived in the house had made their own shortcut down to the river. He turned away from the water and walked on until he came to a rough track winding its way down between the trees and bushes. He ran his fingers through his hair and brushed down his clothes, then swallowed nervously and wiped his sweaty palms on his jeans. A whiskery face peered at him from the bushes. He crouched down. "Stay here," he whispered urgently. "You and Freya have to wait here."

He stood up and stepped off the main path on to the narrow dirt track, hoping no one would be upset about him using this private way in. A rustle in the bushes told him that Baldur had no intention of being left behind and he gave up trying to keep a lid on his own nervousness. Instead, he let it flow out of him. Baldur gave a long, low growl.

For the first time, Robbie made a conscious effort to dominate the link between him and the cat. It wasn't easy to think of some kind of message that might make his intentions clear, but he did his best, sending a picture of himself going inside the house and then another image of him returning to the path beside the river. "You have to stay here," he repeated. "It's not safe for you. Just wait. I'll come back."

He opened the back gate and stepped inside, grateful that somehow he must have made his thoughts clear. Baldur made no attempt to follow, though he could still feel the cat's uneasiness all the way up the garden path.

He had been half hoping that no one was in, but there were lights on in the kitchen. Peering through the window, he saw a round, motherly looking woman busy peeling vegetables at the sink. She wasn't alone. A girl sat at the kitchen table, tossing an apple from hand to hand.

The girl looked a little bit older than Robbie, but he knew that lots of the girls in his class looked older than the boys. She was talking, her face animated, eyes sparkling and whatever she was telling the woman, it was something exciting. The woman turned and said something. Robbie saw the girl jump to her feet, give the woman a quick hug and run out of the room.

Robbie was filled with a sudden, unexpected longing for his father. He swallowed hard to get rid of the lump in his throat, uncomfortably aware that he was spying on someone else's private life, and looked away. There was a climbing frame in the garden. There must be younger children living here too.

Dredging up every scrap of courage he possessed, Robbie walked up to the kitchen door and forced himself to raise his hand and knock. After all, he reminded himself, what was the worst that could happen? Stella Loomis could either send him away, or phone his father. And he would probably have to do that anyway, if she refused to talk to him.

The woman opened the door and stared at Robbie in surprise. She was clearly unused to people arriving at the back of the house instead of the front door.

"Are you Stella Loomis?" Robbie blushed at the quaver in his voice. "I'm ..."

"I know who you are." Her voice was flat. She

looked at him a moment longer, her expression unreadable, then stepped to one side. "I suppose you'd better come in."

Stella didn't invite him to sit down, so he remained where he was, just inside the door, letting the warmth of the kitchen seep into his bones while she leaned back against the sink, arms folded, and gave him a long stare.

At last she spoke. "Your father promised me this would never happen." Robbie thought he saw a flash of fear in her eyes. "And then I get a phone call to tell me you're probably on your way."

"Please ... I don't want to be a nuisance. I just want to ask you a couple of things."

She frowned as he hurried on, hating himself for wilting in the face of her obvious discomfort. He wished now that he'd spent a little more time thinking about what he was going to say. This woman had worked in the lab along with his mother. They had both had babies at the same time. Somehow he had persuaded himself that maybe that other child shared his link with Baldur.

"I wanted to know ... has your daughter ... or son ... ever ..." he tailed off as her expression changed from anger to puzzlement.

"I don't see what my children have to do with you." Her frown deepened, then understanding dawned in her eyes. "I should have guessed," she said finally "Michael was always such a coward. Has he told you anything? About how you were born? About Jane?"

Robbie blinked. "Told me what? I know my mother died when I was born."

Stella took a deep breath and he braced himself for whatever was coming. He wasn't sure he wanted to hear it.

"Jane didn't die in childbirth, Robbie. She died of motor neurone disease."

At Robbie's baffled look, she swallowed hard, then let the words rush out as though she didn't want to think about what she was saying.

"Her muscles wasted away. Eventually, her heart gave out. Jane knew she couldn't have children. Not without the risk of giving it to them."

Robbie's heart thumped and his legs threatened to crumple beneath him. He stared at Stella Loomis in horror. Was this the secret his father had been so determined to keep? Did he have the disease that killed his mother?

Stella guessed what he was thinking and shook her head. "No, Robbie. She didn't pass it on to you. When she found out about the disease, she had her own eggs stored so she could work on them in the lab. She wanted to replace her damaged gene with a different one. Jane was an expert in gene therapy."

A burst of laughter sounded from somewhere in the house and she looked at the kitchen door, then back at Robbie.

"It's not my place to tell you all this," she said. "You need to talk to your father."

"No!" Robbie took a step towards her. "I want you to tell me. I won't leave unless you do!"

Once again, Stella glanced anxiously at the door. Robbie watched as she bit her lip, unable to make up her mind.

At last she said, "I suppose you have a right to know." She turned away from him, looking out the window at the sky, deepening from blue to violet as the day drew to a close. "Jane couldn't make it work, but she couldn't face the thought that she would never have a child of her own. So she linked her replacement gene with the Hox gene from the lab and put them both in ... and it worked." Stella took a deep breath and moved to face him. "You carry the Hox gene, Robbie, just like all the animals she worked on in the lab."

"Me?" Robbie's legs finally gave up under the weight of one shock after another. He made it to a chair and sank down, his thoughts scrabbling first one way, then another as though looking for a way out. There was something that didn't fit. At last he managed to track it down. He looked up at Stella. "But how could she have a baby? If she was so ill?"

There was a long pause. Then Stella spoke again. Her voice sounded as though it came from very far away, filled with a sympathy that hadn't been there before. "I wanted to help her, Robbie. I agreed to carry her baby ... to be a surrogate mother. I was the one who gave birth to you. There never was any other child."

Robbie slumped back in the chair, unable to take it in. A vague memory of a TV news report floated through his head ... about a woman who had had a baby for someone else and then refused to give it up. She must have been a surrogate mother, like Stella had been for him.

"Dad never told me," he whispered. "He never told me anything."

Stella reached out a hand, but withdrew it before it touched him. "I suppose he was afraid to, Robbie. What Jane did was dangerous for everyone. If anyone had found out, the Institute would have been closed down. Everyone would have lost not just their jobs, but their whole career." Her voice grew harsher. "Jane never told me about the Hox gene until it was too late. I was her friend, but she lied to me. She used me like an experimental animal. She tried to tell me later that she was sure it was safe ... that the Hox gene hadn't made any difference to the lab animals, but I don't think she cared whether it did or didn't. She just wanted a baby."

Robbie said nothing. There was nothing to say.

"I'm sorry," she whispered. "You're not my son." Her voice dropped even lower, but Robbie heard her all the same. "I'm not even sure you're completely human."

He staggered to his feet and made to leave, too shocked and confused to question her insistence that he should go out the front door, not the back. He followed her down a hall littered with the evidence of family life; muddy boots and jackets, a mountain bike propped against one wall. From behind a closed door, he could hear children's voices shouting over the noise of the television. But he knew now there was no one in there like him, no one turning their head, puzzled by the faint trace of another mind somewhere near the river. That other child had been nothing but a fantasy.

Robbie wanted no more answers. He had had more than enough already. He reached the front door, taking great gulps of cold air, and stumbled blindly towards the gate, aware of nothing except the need to escape. But he barely managed two steps along the pavement before someone grabbed hold of his arms and he looked up to see his father's face bending towards him.

Chapter 12

Michael blinked, bleary-eyed. "I must have fallen asleep in the car," he said. "I was up all last night." He glanced at the house. "She wouldn't let me wait inside. I've been sitting out here for hours. I've been so worried ..."

Robbie stepped away from him. He saw understanding dawn in his father's eyes.

"Stella told you, didn't she? Oh, Robbie, you mustn't blame your mother. She ..."

"This hasn't got anything to do with my *mother.*" Robbie glared at him. "She's not the one who lied to me all my life." He jerked a thumb in the direction of the house. "Is she right? Was it all just to save your stupid job?"

His father reached out. "Robbie, you must know that's not true! I don't understand how you could think that."

Robbie slapped his hand away. "But I do understand! I understand you're nothing but a liar and a cheat!" The words rasped out, his throat raw with the effort of holding back the tears. "You lied to me all my life and you're lying now!"

Michael followed Robbie's pointing finger down the street and frowned in confusion when he saw Gavin Moir hurrying towards them, his face grim and determined. He turned back to his son.

"Robbie, please ... I swear I didn't know! I didn't tell him you'd be here! He must have followed me!"

Robbie pushed out with both hands, sending his father stumbling into the fence then he turned and ran, desperate to get away, to find somewhere he could hide from everyone and everything.

He dashed down the path at the side of the house, and saw the two cats standing side by side, waiting. Baldur moved to one side and Robbie brushed past. A shiver ran up his spine as the cat's coiled tension flooded through him, but nothing could stop his headlong rush across the bridge and up the slope on the other side.

The cats moved together, blocking the path. Robbie knew there was no way either of the men could pass them. He heard the sound of running footsteps behind him falter and then stop.

At last Robbie reached the shelter of the trees and staggered on.

Branches whipped his face and snagged his clothing, leaving bright beads of blood across his forehead and his hands, but he didn't stop, not until his feet snagged on a twisting mass of roots and he fell heavily to the ground, panting for breath.

Robbie stared down at his hands. His human hands, Then he gave a great sob and smacked his fist against the trunk of a gnarled and twisted elm, his mind seething with hatred for Joe and Gavin Moir, for Stella Loomis and, most of all, for the father who had never wanted a son, but had kept him close for fear that someone would find out what his wife had done.

Eventually, the tears stopped. Robbie sat up and rubbed his face, then he pushed himself further into the shelter of the knotty roots and sat with his arms around his knees, his head bent.

His mother hadn't given birth to him. She had created him — a child with the Hox genes. He didn't want to be different. If he could, he would rip out everything within him that didn't fit. But that wasn't possible. Stella Loomis seemed to think there were bits of him that weren't human. But he didn't know which bits those were. He didn't even know what the Hox gene was *for.* Robbie was suddenly swamped by a feeling of utter loneliness. There was no one else like him anywhere in the world.

But that wasn't quite true, was it? Robbie shifted uneasily. Joe had said that Baldur, too, had the Hox gene. They were both "freaks." The only difference was that they wanted to keep Baldur in a cage. He frowned, recognising the presence inside his head. It was distant still, but growing stronger all the time. Robbie clenched his fists. Surely Baldur must know he didn't want him near.

Go away! Leave me alone! The thought was backed by all the force of Robbie's misery and anger.

But Baldur didn't seem interested. Something else was taking up too much of his attention. Robbie lifted his head from his knees, listening, but not with his ears. The cats weren't following *him*, at least not directly. Somebody was tracing the path Robbie had followed on his flight through the woods. And whoever it was, the cats were behind them. Robbie sat up. In Baldur at least, he could sense the intense concentration of a hunter stalking his prey.

It could be his father, or Gavin Moir. Or maybe it was Joe. Well, he told himself with a last burst of anger and grief, if he wasn't human, then he owed nothing to anyone.

But he knew he was fooling himself. Baldur was afraid of people. Left to himself, he was no risk to anyone. It was because of the threat to Robbie that Baldur was hunting. He was trying to protect Robbie in the only way he knew.

Using the trunk of the tree to lever himself to his feet, Robbie stood up. He wasn't an animal. He *was* human. He had to stop Baldur. He couldn't allow Baldur to hurt someone, even to protect himself. Wearily, he set off, back the way he had come, using the thread inside his head to guide him.

As the link grew in strength, he found himself slipping into the cat's mind with alarming ease. But it wasn't Baldur who was leading the hunt. It was Freya. Baldur had never learned the necessary skills. But he was learning them now. He followed Freya through the bushes, moving as silently as she did. Robbie felt sick. The two cats were tracking their victim, waiting for the perfect moment to attack.

He tried to urge Baldur to stop, but it was no good. The cat was totally focused on the hunt. Robbie increased his pace, desperate to reach the cats before their perfect moment arrived, knowing that even if he did manage to stop Baldur, there was no way he could stop Freya.

But he didn't give up trying to reach Baldur, battering at the cat's consciousness until at last, with a huge surge of relief, he knew that his panic had finally broken through Baldur's intense concentration. He felt the cat falter.

As Baldur's mind embraced his, he felt the world spin out of focus. For the second time in his life, he saw through Baldur's eyes. A tall, gangling figure was moving out of the shelter of the trees into more open space. He forced the vision away and increased his speed, running faster than he ever had before, his breath rasping in his throat, knowing all the time that it was hopeless. He wasn't going to make it.

"No," he sobbed. "Please, no!"

There was still no sign of any clearing ahead, and he had no idea how much further he had to go. Black spots floated in front of his eyes and his exhausted body screamed at him to stop. Heedless of any obstacles in his path he ran on, stumbling over fallen branches and hidden rocks, forcing air into his toiling lungs until he thought they would surely burst.

He finally erupted from the trees to find himself in a clearing littered with freshly cut logs, running towards a ragged stranger who walked slowly and confidently forward, clearly unaware that Freya had now abandoned her stealthy approach in favour of a bounding lope, every muscle and every sense locked on to her intended victim.

Robbie charged forward, waving his arms wildly, yelling as loudly as he could. Confused, Freya veered away, running in a wide arc that brought her back towards her target. Robbie screamed her name, but it was hopeless. She was ready to take her victim down. Nothing could stop her now.

Then he saw Baldur erupt out of the bushes, leaping high in the air. He landed on Freya hard enough to knock her flat on the ground and the two cats rolled over in a spitting, snarling confusion of teeth and claws.

Hearing the noise the man glanced behind him. Then he looked back at Robbie and laughed a little wildly.

"I knew you'd turn up," he said.

But Robbie didn't answer. He wasn't looking at the man's face. All his attention was focused on the wicked-looking knife glittering in one filthy hand.

Chapter 13

Robbie watched the knife while the man watched Robbie. Neither paid any attention to the two cats. Freya was scrabbling backwards away from Baldur, her lips curled back in a snarl, lashing out at him furiously.

Robbie took one step back and stopped, halted by a pile of brushwood at his back. He must have vaulted over it without even noticing. At last he found his voice.

"What do you want?" It was hard to look the man in the face and still concentrate on the knife.

The man wiped his nose on his sleeve. He grinned in a friendly fashion, but Robbie didn't like the gleam in his eye.

"I've been following you ... and your friends." It was odd how he ignored the cats. He must be able to hear them thrashing around behind him. But he only seemed interested in Robbie.

He finally noticed Robbie's constant glances at the knife and his eyebrows lifted in sudden comprehension. "Ah, no." He laughed. "Don't worry. It's not for you." He gestured behind him. "It's for them."

"Don't!" said Robbie, suddenly aware that Baldur was reacting to his fear of the knife. "Put it down!"

As Callum lowered the knife, Robbie collapsed with a thump on the pile of damp, moss-covered branches and looked at Baldur, who was now trying to lick Freya's face. She kept turning her head away. Clearly, she was not at all happy.

The man moved closer and Robbie wrinkled his nose at the smell that wafted towards him — a combination of unwashed body and wood smoke. The face behind the matted beard was as brown as a nut and his hair, which was stiff with dirt, looked as though it had been hacked off with a knife.

The stranger held out a grubby hand. "Good to meet you. I'm Callum."

Robbie heard a lilt in the man's voice that told him he wasn't from around here, but from somewhere much further north, maybe even the islands.

"I'm Robbie." Unwillingly, he shook hands, resisting the urge to wipe his own afterwards. Even though the knife was no longer pointed in his direction, there was something about the intensity of the man's bright blue eyes that made him uncomfortable,

"It's okay," said Callum. "You can trust me. I'm into animal rights as well." His forehead creased in a puzzled frown. "Are you by yourself? What happened to your folks?"

"I'm not ..." Robbie clamped his mouth shut, realising just in time that it was much safer to let the man believe there were people somewhere who cared about him.

Callum tapped the side of his nose with a grimy finger and winked. "Doing this yourself, are you? Well, good for you." He leaned forward. Robbie held his breath.

"Those cats are smart. I watched them. They kept those two guys at the bridge long enough to let you get away. Then they took off after you. I thought I was following *them,* but I must have got in front somehow."

Robbie knew that had been no accident. The cats must have circled round behind him. "Did the men come after them?"

Callum sniffed. "Dunno. Last I saw of them, they were arguing. Fighting, really."

So Gavin Moir didn't get a chance to use the tranquillizer gun. Robbie wasn't sure if he was glad or sorry.

"How long have you been following me?"

"All day. I saw what happened at the motorway this morning."

So Baldur had been right. Someone had been following them. But not Gavin Moir. It gave Robbie a jolt to realize that it was only yesterday morning that he had set off on his first attempt at skipping school. It felt as though a thousand years had passed.

Callum flicked the hand holding the knife in the direction of the cats and Robbie tensed as Baldur raised his head.

"It was the cats I was watching. But then I realized." His eyes narrowed. "It wasn't just the cats ... it's you. They treat you like one of them. There's something special about you."

"Special?" Robbie swallowed nervously.

The man shrugged. "We can talk about that later. Right now, we need to make sure you can't be followed. Those cats are carrying chips. We have to get them out."

"Chips?" Robbie knew he was beginning to sound like a parrot, but it was hard to keep up with this odd stranger, who jumped from one thing to another without any explanation in between.

"You know ..." Callum said with a hint of impatience. "Computer chips. That's how they can track you. They do it with most captive animals nowadays, just in case someone decides to *liberate* them. They usually put them in the shoulder."

Robbie felt a sudden surge of relief. So that was the source of Gavin Moir's uncanny ability to track them down. Nothing more than a simple piece of technology.

He watched as Callum turned round to look at the cats, now lying quietly side-by-side. Baldur, as usual, had his eyes fixed on Robbie.

Robbie knew by now that wherever he went, the cats would follow. Callum was right. If he didn't want to be found, then the chips had to come out.

Clambering wearily to his feet, Robbie crossed the clearing and crouched down beside Baldur and Freya. He blinked nervously, wondering how he could possibly persuade them to let Callum use his knife. If the cats thought he was trying to hurt them, it would be disastrous.

Freya leaned forward and licked his hand. She no longer had any fear of him. Not yet anyway. As smoothly as he could, he reached past her, placed his hand on Baldur's shoulder and ran his fingers across the soft, warm fur, feeling the muscle beneath. Robbie remembered his father telling him all animals were the same under the skin; the same blood and muscle and bone. Only the tiniest difference in the DNA was needed to form the shape of a cat or a boy. He pushed the thought away as his searching fingers found a small, hard lump. He looked up at Callum.

"You were right," he said. "It's here."

Callum knelt down beside him, the knife ready in his hand.

"Wait a minute." Robbie looked into Baldur's eyes, sending a picture of Joe inserting something beneath Baldur's skin, trying to turn the thought into a question. The cat gave a low growl.

"This has to come out," said Robbie, keeping his voice gentle, still stroking Baldur's fur. "Otherwise they can find you any time they like." He sent another picture, this time of Callum using the knife to remove the lump.

"Do it now," he said.

Callum's stroke was swift. He made only one small cut, dug beneath the skin and twisted the knife, flipping the chip out from beneath the fur. Baldur turned his head to lick the blood that trickled from his shoulder. It was that easy. Robbie took hold of Freya, stroking her slowly to reassure her.

Freya looked up in surprise as the knife pricked her flesh, but the chip was out before she had any time to react. Baldur leaned over and rubbed his face against hers, but she shrugged him off, stalked a few paces away and flopped down again with an air of outraged irritation that brought a bubble of laughter rising in Robbie's throat. Callum unfolded a grimy hand to reveal two black discs, red and slippery. Robbie was surprised at how small they were.

"State of the art, these." Callum dropped the

chips on the ground and stood up. "That's it then," he said. "The cats disappear right here."

"Thanks." Robbie didn't know where he was going next, but it didn't really matter, as long as he was nowhere near the discarded chips. He knew he ought to be on his feet and away as soon as possible, but somehow he just couldn't seem to persuade his body to start moving.

Callum looked at him thoughtfully. "Have you got someplace to go?"

Robbie shrugged. "Not really."

"You can stay with me for a bit, if you want."

Like everyone else, Robbie had been warned of the dangers of trusting a stranger, but that felt like a different world now. He had no place else to go, no one he could trust to take him in. "Okay." He nodded wearily, knowing that none of the warnings applied to him. Not now he had a fierce and deadly guardian who seemed more than willing to destroy anyone who threatened him.

Callum studied him for a moment, then reached into a pocket and pulled out a bar of chocolate. "Here."

It was still in its wrapper, bent and crumpled, but untouched. Robbie wolfed it down then struggled to his feet, hoping he wouldn't have to walk too far.

Robbie toiled up the slope behind Callum. He didn't need to look behind him to know that the cats were following. Moving in and out of the trees, always climbing, his muscles aching with the strain, until eventually the trees gave way to bushes. Gradually the bushes thinned out and they were walking over coarse grass on bare, open hillside.

Robbie looked around nervously, but there was no one in sight.

"Most people keep to the tracks," Callum spoke over his shoulder as they crossed the ridge and dropped down into a corrie on the other side. "No one comes this way very often. Except me."

Robbie picked his way down, struggling for balance as his feet skidded on loose rock. If he fell, he probably wouldn't be able to get back up again.

"Took them from the wild, did they? You can tell." Callum was watching Freya's confident progress down the rock-strewn hillside.

"Freya's from Norway," said Robbie. "But Baldur ..." he clamped his mouth shut. It didn't seem like a good idea to say what Baldur was. The cat still limped a little, but there was a new confidence in the way he moved. He was a very different creature from the one that had struggled to cross a fence, or had flinched away from the flight of a bird. Robbie shrugged. "I don't know where Baldur's from."

At the far end of the corrie, Callum began to climb back up again. Robbie looked at the slope and almost decided to give up. Eventually he made it to the top, mostly on his hands and knees, to find Callum sitting on a rock waiting for him.

"Not much further." He waved one arm towards an even higher hill. Halfway up, a stand of birch trees huddled together, sharing protection from the wind. "We'll be stopping in the trees. We don't have to go all the way to the top."

Robbie said nothing. He had no energy left for speech. He simply staggered to the edge of the hill, slid all the way down it on his backside and squelched across the boggy bottom of the next valley. He pulled himself up the slope by grabbing hold of one tree branch after another until he caught up with Callum, who pointed out a narrow split in the rocky hillside, which was hidden from view by the sheltering trees.

"Here we are," he said. "Home sweet home." Then he bent his head and disappeared inside.

Chapter 14

Robbie stepped into the dark space between the stones. He felt someone take hold of his elbow and guide him forward, until his knees bumped against a shelf of rock.

"Sit." Callum's voice floated out of the darkness.

Obediently, Robbie dropped down. The stone seat was unexpectedly soft, carpeted with springy branches and covered in what felt like a rough blanket. His eyelids drooped as he watched Callum adding wood to a glowing pile of embers in the middle of the floor. The cats were still outside. He could feel Baldur's anxiety, and his desire to urge an unwilling Freya inside the cave, but he had no strength left to care.

"Drink this."

Robbie jerked awake to see Callum looming over him. In the shadows beyond the fire he caught the glint of two pairs of eyes. So ... the cats were here as well. It was a struggle to keep his eyes open as he took a wooden bowl from Callum's hands and raised it to his lips. He gulped down something warm and savoury, then he sank on to the blanket, the bowl tumbling from his hands. He didn't even hear it hit the ground.

A woman was looking down at him. With the instant understanding that comes in dreams, Robbie knew she was his mother. He opened his mouth to tell her she couldn't be here, that she was dead, and was horrified to hear an animal growl issue from his throat. He saw her smile in satisfaction as she blurred and melted into another, more familiar shape. Michael Bruce stared down at Robbie then melted away with no hint of recognition in his eyes. As the tall, stork-like figure turned and walked away into the flickering firelight, he opened his mouth again. He strained the muscles in his throat to the limit, but the words would not come.

"No! Wait!" Robbie jerked awake with a suddenness that left him gasping for breath. He sat up, looking wildly around. Callum was hunched over the fire, feeding the flames from a small stock of broken branches.

"I thought you were never going to wake up."

Robbie rubbed his face, ran his fingers through his hair and shook his head. "What time is it?"

Callum shrugged. "Don't know. But you've slept for a day and a night." He unfolded his legs and stood up. "Don't worry. Your friends are outside somewhere. Hunting. But they'll be back"

So the cats were still with him. But at least they were far enough away to keep his mind free from their need to kill and eat.

With that thought, Robbie realized he was ravenous. He watched Callum spoon something from the small pot that hung over the fire and walk over to give it to him. He forced himself to eat slowly, relishing the hot, meaty broth while Callum crouched nearby, staring at him with unnerving intensity.

"Toilet's outside," he said, when Robbie was finished.

"There are people looking for me ... and the cats," said Robbie. By now, they must have combed every inch of this area. And they'll do it again and again, until they find what they're looking for.

"Don't worry about it." Callum grinned. "I went back and picked up the chips. Took them to a garage and dumped them in the back of a truck heading south. They've got a lot of ground to cover."

For the first time in days, Robbie felt himself relax. Eventually, Moir would backtrack to where he last saw the cats, but that wouldn't be for a while at least. He grinned at Callum, stood up on his aching legs and tottered outside. He had no trouble finding the trench. All he had to do was follow the smell.

As he headed back to join Callum beside the fire, he sensed Baldur moving closer on a wave of welcome and delight. A moment later the two cats trotted through the narrow opening. Baldur made straight for Robbie, nudging him enthusiastically, rasping his tongue across his face.

Robbie pushed him away. Baldur dropped to the sandy floor beside Freya and began his cleaning routine while Robbie watched enviously, wishing he could clean himself as easily as the cats.

"Is there any water to wash with?"

"Water has to be carried up here," snapped Callum, not bothering to look up. "There's none to spare."

Robbie blushed. He had assumed the man was dirty because he wasn't interested in keeping clean. "Sorry."

"You won't notice after a while."

Robbie's cheerfulness evaporated. Callum was

right, he thought gloomily. What difference did it make if he was clean or dirty? He was stuck here on this hillside with nowhere to go.

Callum turned back to face him. "Who's Gavin Moir?"

Robbie bit his lip, wondering how much he had given away during his dark dreams. He cringed at the thought of Callum looking at him as though he was an alien creature, not human at all.

He nodded towards the cat. "Gavin Moir is the man I took *them* from." He pointed at the cats. "Baldur and Freya."

Callum nodded slowly. "The God of Fire killed him, you know."

Robbie nodded back, anxious to keep Callum happy, but his confusion must have shown. Callum leaned forward, his eyes alight.

"Do you know them, Robbie? Have you read the sagas? Do you know about Allfather Odin and the Fenris Wolf? The Midgard Serpent?"

Robbie shook his head and reality flickered back into Callum's eyes. "No," he said. "Of course you haven't. You're just a kid." He glanced over at the cats and lowered his voice as if he thought they might understand his words. "Freya, mother of us all. And Baldur the Beautiful ..."

Baldur looked up at the sound of his name.

"Loki was jealous of Baldur's grace and beauty," Callum went on. "That's us, Robbie. We are the children of Loki. No other animal uses fire."

A shiver ran down Robbie's spine. At any other time, or in any other place, he might have laughed. But here, in this hole under the hill, it was all too easy to see that Callum believed what he was saying.

Callum turned back to the cats. “Baldur and Freya,” he whispered. “The old gods have come back to earth.”

“They’re not gods!” Robbie squirmed away from Callum and his wild talk.

“I’m not mad, you know,” Callum said with a smile. “Well, only as mad as you get if you live on your own.”

Baldur was now staring at Callum with a fixed glare that made Robbie nervous. He had picked up Robbie’s uneasiness. He clamped down on it firmly, hoping to calm the cat down.

“You know, Robbie” Callum went on, unaware of the invisible struggle taking place between boy and cat, “I was a student once. Biochemistry.” He frowned. “They said I couldn’t cope. But they were wrong. That wasn’t the problem.”

He leaned forward with fierce intensity. Robbie stared into eyes that glittered like chips of ice, unable to look away.

“The trouble was, I could see further than they could. I knew what was really going on.” He jerked a thumb towards the cave entrance. “Those trees out there are just about all that’s left of a forest that once covered the whole world. Men started with stone axes and finished the job with chainsaws. And then, when the trees were gone, they began to burrow under the ground for coal and metal.”

Robbie stared at the spittle gathering in the corners of Callum’s mouth. An inner voice warned him to be very, very careful. Baldur shifted uneasily and let out a long, low growl. But Callum didn't notice. All his attention was on Robbie.

"I thought it was too late." Callum said. "But I was wrong. I should have had more faith. Because now, the old gods have returned. The ones who know how to live in harmony with the earth."

Robbie flinched as Callum leaned forward and tapped him on the chest.

"You, Robbie. You are one of them."

"I'm not a god! I'm just a boy!" Robbie heard the quaver in his voice and struggled to control his fear. If this man ever found out that Robbie and Baldur were created in one of the laboratories he clearly hated so much, it might tip him over the edge.

Callum shook his head. "I watched you ... remember? You and the cats. They seem to know when you're hungry. Or angry. Or afraid. And you read them the same way. You read their messages just as they read yours. No ordinary person can do that."

"I didn't do anything special. I just let them out," Robbie said urgently. "That's all I did ... and then they followed me."

But Callum wasn't listening. "When I was a boy," he said thoughtfully, "my father told me that animals are ours to do with as we please. As far as I know he still thinks that's true." The dreamy look vanished and his eyes flashed with anger. "But my father was wrong! We are all animals. And I *knew* that some day I would find someone like you. Someone made the way we were meant to be."

Callum shuffled closer. Robbie could smell him — a combination of dirt, wood smoke and unwashed body.

"Do you know what my father would call you?"

Wordlessly, Robbie shook his head.

"Abomination." Callum spoke so softly that Robbie had to strain to hear him. "He would call you Abomination. Humans and animals were not meant to be equal." Callum reached out and laid a filthy finger on Robbie's chest. "But I know what you really are."

Robbie swallowed. He couldn't speak. Baldur rose silently to his feet. Robbie knew that if Callum tried to touch him again, it would be the last thing he ever did.

"I don't know how it happened, but you're like the first people." Callum said softly, "You are the kind of human I hope to be."

Horrified, Robbie leaned away from Callum's filthy face and crooked smile.

"No," he whispered. "I'm not like you."

Chapter 15

After his outburst, Callum retreated into silence, except for a muttered order not to let the fire die down too far. He reclaimed his bed and was soon snoring loudly, leaving Robbie alone beside the fire.

Warm. Baldur's thought trickled into Robbie's head. He hunched closer to the fire, turning away from the cat, but a bump on his back almost sent him sprawling as Baldur settled close beside him. And Robbie couldn't deny he made a comfortable barrier against the draughts that fanned the flames and sent shadows dancing across the walls.

Two days of little food and gruelling cross-country walking had left him weak and exhausted. Thanks to Callum's trick with the tracking chips, there was time to rest, but Robbie knew that this was no more than a temporary shelter. At the moment, Callum was on his side, but Robbie saw how he frowned as he carefully divided the food, how he saved every scrap that might be useful. Sometimes, too, he seemed to forget that Robbie was there until something jolted him back to the here and now.

"I can't stay here," he murmured drowsily. But he was too tired to think about it. As the cat's purr reverberated through his body, he slid down on to the sandy floor.

For the first three days, Robbie did almost nothing except sleep. With food and rest, his body began to recover, but he couldn't control his mind so easily. Each night he lay beside the fire, struggling to stay awake until Callum's rumbling snore announced that he could no longer eavesdrop on Robbie's haunted dreams.

As his strength returned, his spirits rose, but only if he was careful to keep his thoughts away from the events of the last few days. He occupied himself instead with an idea that gradually grew into a definite plan. He knew what he had to do. He was going home. Not to that boxy little house in Duncraig, but to his own house, deep in the woods of Appin. It was a long walk, but it didn't matter how long he took.

They would probably come looking for him there, but that didn't matter. He would find someplace nearby and wait them out. And when they were gone, he would reclaim the house for himself.

It occurred to him that his grandmother must have known what her daughter had done. Maybe she had left the house to him because she knew that one day Robbie would need a refuge. It was a comforting thought.

He even began to hope that he could persuade Baldur to stay with Callum. The cats were gaining in strength and endurance, roaming the hills and the woodland in search of rabbits. They would be free, but Callum would be here to help them if they needed it. Callum thought both cats were like Freya, animals rescued from the wild, and Robbie was careful to say nothing that might suggest otherwise. Instead, he told Callum that the cats were not going to be released into the wild, but were intended for a breeding programme in a zoo.

Callum's voice thrilled with enthusiasm as he explained why the cats should be allowed to roam free. It was part of the balance of nature, he said. They did a better job than people.

"A human hunter finds his deer ..." he raised an imaginary rifle and squinted down the barrel. "Maybe he'll leave a doe with its fawn, but otherwise, he doesn't care." He pulled the trigger with a slow click of his tongue. "Cats don't hunt like that. They don't go after the ones who might put up a fight. And when the weak and the lame are gone, there's more for the rest of the deer to eat. It's good for the deer, Robbie, as well as the cats."

Callum had said he was once a student. He certainly seemed to know a lot about animals. Robbie took a chance.

"Have you ever heard of Hox genes?"

Callum's eyes grew watchful and Robbie tensed, afraid he had said the wrong thing.

"Where did you hear about them?"

"My Dad told me something about them but I can't remember what they do," Robbie said quickly.

"Yes," said Callum, his face brightening. "We had them once — many more than we do now."

"What are they for?" Robbie kept his voice steady, afraid of betraying too much interest.

"They control growth." Callum waved an arm vaguely in the air. "Arms, legs, brain ... that sort of thing. Humans used to have more, but we lost them, maybe because we learned to talk and use tools. But other animals still have them." He was twitching with excitement. "Maybe that's the miracle, Robbie. Maybe you were born with the genes we lost so long ago! Look at how you communicate with the cats!"

"Maybe." This was getting too close to the truth for comfort. Robbie stood up. "I'd better fetch some firewood."

He walked away, aware of Callum's eyes following him hungrily all the way across the cave.

Days ran one into the other and Robbie's legs grew steadily more used to tramping the hills, helping Callum gather firewood and herbs for the pot, but he never travelled too far from the cave and Callum never invited him on his on longer trips in search of food. He did not hunt, he explained to Robbie. He only took what others had already killed and abandoned. Robbie soon discovered it was not only the cats who dined on road kill.

Late one afternoon, Robbie sat by the fire, watching Callum mix dough and flour into a paste, then wrap it round a stick and hold it over the fire.

Outside, a chill wind was blowing steadily across the hills. Robbie was surprised to realize that it must have been almost two weeks since he stumbled into the cave and collapsed, exhausted, on Callum's bed. It was fully autumn now, with winter just around the corner.

"The cats are happy here," he said tentatively.

"Yes but if anyone sees them, they'll be shot," said Callum. He laughed and Robbie saw the wild look appear in his eyes. "Better a short life and a happy one, eh?"

"The cats know how to stay out of sight," said Robbie. "But I can't stay here." He was careful to shield his thoughts from Baldur, who lay somewhere in the shadows with Freya, sleeping off a successful hunt. "You won't be able to feed me all through the winter."

"No," agreed Callum. "I can't." He peeled the bread carefully from the stick and handed it to Robbie. "Will you go home? I suppose your folks will be glad to see you." There was a wistful note in his voice. Clearly, Callum did not expect that kind of welcome from his own family.

"No." Robbie tossed the hot bread from hand to hand until it was cool enough to eat. "I don't want to go home. I'm going north. To Appin."

He had picked his moment carefully, expecting an argument, but to his surprise, Callum didn't seem to be bothered at the thought of Robbie setting off alone across the hills, just as the weather was turning cold. Instead, he bubbled with enthusiasm, suggesting different routes and places where Robbie could find shelter.

"The easiest route is by the Pass of Brander." Callum pointed to the map he had drawn on the sandy floor. "But you can't get through on foot. There's only the main road and cliffs on either side. And anyway, you can't cross Loch Etive without a boat." He scratched his head thoughtfully. "You'll have to head north-west, down into the glen and then over Etive Mor. There's two roads to cross before Glen Etive — one at Crianlarich and the other at Tyndrum. I suppose you'd rather not be seen?"

Robbie nodded.

"Then you'll have to get past both roads in one night. But that shouldn't be too difficult. They're only about five miles apart."

He made it sound so easy. "Glen Etive," Robbie said thoughtfully, remembering a summer day when he and Dad were travelling north. They had decided to stop in Glen Etive for lunch, but they lasted less than five minutes before dense clouds of tiny stinging insects chased them back to the car. He smiled up at Callum. "Midges."

"Not at this time of year. It's too cold."

Robbie's smile evaporated.

"I can help you, though," said Callum. He jumped to his feet and hurried towards one of the gaps in the rock wall where he stored his meagre possessions. He rummaged around for a moment then threw something over his shoulder before he rushed off to another of his hiding places.

Robbie looked down at the ancient, mildewed backpack at his feet. Something else came flying out of the darkness and he struggled to free himself from a filthy piece of heavy duty plastic.

"These will keep you warm." Callum dumped a pile of smelly rabbit skins at Robbie's feet. "And so will this." Triumphantly, he waved a Black Watch cap in the air. Robbie stared up at the musty thing, unable to share his glee.

"Beggars can't be choosers," Callum said roughly, throwing the cap on top of the pile of furs.

Robbie saw the hurt in his eyes. "Thanks, Callum," he said humbly, but Callum only shrugged and turned away.

Later, Robbie sat outside, watching the evening sun sink behind the trees. He knew Callum was right. He *was* a beggar. He had no right to feel so disgusted by Callum or his life. At least he knew how to survive.

The breeze tugged a shower of leaves from the branches, scattering them across the ground. Robbie sighed. He still didn't have any clear idea of how to persuade Baldur to stay behind. Maybe he didn't really want to. He had nothing now — no mother, a father who didn't want him — who had never wanted him. Stella Loomis was right. He had no place in the human world. All he had was the cats.

Robbie.

He froze. It was the first time Baldur had used his name. He looked up to see the cat sitting close by, his spotted coat almost invisible in the dappled light. A shaft of sunlight transformed the fallen beech leaves into piles of gold, a vast treasure piled in drifts on the forest floor.

Stay, Robbie. Stay.

Robbie stared into Baldur's golden eyes. This was more than thoughts passed from mind to mind. Baldur had understood everything that had passed between Callum and Robbie. He could understand speech.

And Baldur was waiting for an answer.

At last, Robbie found his voice. "I can't stay here."

There was a long silence. Then he heard the voice again in his head.

You go. We go.

"No," said Robbie. "I won't take you with me."

Chapter 16

Hox. The word slipped into Robbie's head. He clenched his fists until the nails dug into his flesh. There was too much pressure in his life already. And now this. He had built a wall once before. He would do it again.

You cannot, came the voice in his head. *We are one*.

"I don't understand." Robbie sat with his head in his hands. "It's just not possible. This isn't really happening."

Baldur was right. Callum thought that Robbie read all kinds of signals to understand what the cats felt. And maybe that did explain some things, like Freya's willingness to accept his presence. But the link with Baldur was much more than that. Baldur sent not just feelings, but words too. There was only one explanation. Baldur had worked it out already. The thing that Baldur and Robbie shared. The Hox genes.

Yes. Now you understand.

Robbie thought hard. Surely there were loads of other people working on the Hox genes, not just the scientists at the Institute? Did that mean there were others like him? Creatures who could communicate with each other the way he did with Baldur? But then his momentary excitement evaporated. Robbie was twelve years old, Baldur three. Surely by now someone, somewhere would have discovered what Hox genes could do. And even if there were others, there would be no one like him. Scientists weren't allowed to experiment on human beings.

Robbie frowned. It still didn't make sense. Even if Baldur had more than his share of Hox genes, it didn't explain how he could understand human speech.

He shook his head. There was a part of the puzzle still missing. But his visit to Stella Loomis had taught him a bitter lesson — looking for answers was dangerous.

Struck by a sudden thought, he looked up at Baldur. What had his life been like, trapped in a cage, understanding everything that was happening to him?

Baldur padded across and sat down opposite Robbie, staring into his face.

Secret. My secret. Yours, now.

It struck Robbie then that this was the end of his plan to set off on his own. Joe hadn't realized the truth, probably because Baldur was never given the chance to show how much he understood, not when he was trapped inside his cage.

But here, Baldur was free. And although Callum was more than a little strange, he wasn't stupid. Eventually he would realize that the cat understood far more than any normal animal could. If he ever mentioned to anyone that the lynx existed, that it understood speech, then that information might eventually filter back to the Institute. And more than likely, Callum himself would be dragged off to some sterile hospital for treatment. Robbie knew that would destroy him. Callum belonged out here. He looked at Baldur suspiciously. Why had he finally decided to share his secret; that he could understand what people were saying?

We are one.

"No."

Yes!

Robbie pushed the cat away. "Go away," he said. "Leave me alone."

He stayed outside long after dark, until the cold night air finally drove him back to the shelter of the cave. He refused to look at the cats as he stumbled over to the fire and sank down on the ground.

Callum handed him a piece of dried rabbit meat. "I've been thinking," he said. "This isn't the right place for your friends. There are too many farms and roads here. People are going to notice eventually."

Robbie chewed on the tough strip of meat, wondering why it was that no matter how miserable he felt, his stomach still demanded attention. "It's all right," he said between mouthfuls. "I'd thought of that already. I'll have to take them with me."

He pushed away a surge of relief from Baldur. He wasn't doing this for his sake. If anyone ever discovered Baldur's ability to understand speech, then maybe one day they would make the link between him and Robbie. He couldn't afford to take the risk.

"Tomorrow," he said to Callum. "I'll go tomorrow."

Next morning, Callum eyed Robbie with the air of an artist about to start work on a blank canvas.

"What are you wearing underneath?"

Robbie told him, nervously wondering whether Callum planned to force him into some horrible outfit stitched together from stinking rabbit fur.

"Take off the trousers and the extra sweat shirt. Wrap them in this." He handed Robbie a plastic carrier bag.

Robbie found a dark corner of the cave and did as he was told. When he returned, he found Callum surrounded by small piles of different objects. He took the clothes from Robbie and jammed them into the bottom of the backpack.

"Meat," he said, holding up another plastic-wrapped packet. "This will keep you going for a few days, but you'll probably need to find more. And take this." He thrust something into Robbie's hand — a creased and crumpled ten-pound note. "I don't need it."

Robbie knew that wasn't true. Callum did need the money. How else did he get the flour, or the matches he hoarded so carefully? But he also knew it would be an insult to refuse such generosity.

"Thanks," Robbie tucked it away in the inside pocket of his jacket.

Callum opened another plastic bag and spilled some tufts of dried sheep's wool on to the ground. He added one of his precious boxes of matches and rewrapped it carefully. "Chances are, you'll need a fire. It's going to be cold at night on the high ground. You'll have to pick up wood as you go along. There's nothing but rock up there."

Gradually the pack filled with all the things Callum seemed to think Robbie would need — the black plastic sheet for shelter, a bag of food, the kindling and his dry clothes. Then he made Robbie take off his boots and line them with some of the dreaded rabbit fur. The rest went into the bag along with everything else. After that, he dumped the whole lot out on to the ground.

"Now you pack it," he ordered. "You need to know exactly where everything is. You might need to get your hands on something in a hurry. Or in the dark."

When he was finally satisfied, Callum stood up and placed a thick branch on top of the fire. "I'll walk you as far as the top of Ben Ledi."

Robbie shivered in the damp morning air as he climbed up through the trees towards the top of the hill with the cats following close behind. His disgust at being forced to put his feet inside the fur-lined boots gave way to a sense of respect for Callum. The man might be more than a little odd but as far as surviving outdoors was concerned, he knew what he was talking about. The rabbit fur kept Robbie's feet warm and snug in spite of the morning chill.

When the trees gave out, Robbie followed Callum up a slanting path round the curve of the hill, his legs gradually adopting a smooth, regular rhythm. It was reassuring to discover that his time with Callum had left him fit and well rested.

As they moved higher, they found themselves walking into a thick mist that hung low over the ground. Callum nodded in satisfaction.

"That's good. It means we can use the path. I don't think anybody will see us."

Robbie followed Callum as he changed direction, angling more directly up the rough grassy slope. He could see almost nothing beyond the wall of mist, but Callum continued on with confidence, threading his way between massive boulders until he emerged beside a well-worn path. He pointed ahead.

"This takes you straight across the top of Ben Ledi. Then it drops into the next valley." He glanced at Robbie. "Only because of this weather, mind. And you'll still need to keep an eye out."

A chilly wind tugged at the mist, sending pale grey tendrils curling around the rock. Robbie shivered, more from nervous anticipation than cold. Ignoring the flutter in the pit of his stomach, he held out a hand to Callum.

"Thanks Callum. I wouldn't have made it this far without you."

Callum shook his hand, then he shrugged. "If the gods offer you their company, I'm not going to be fool enough to refuse it, am I? It's me that should be thanking you, Robbie."

A flash of doubt appeared in his eyes as he looked at Robbie, as though he had only just noticed how young he was. "Once you're off Ben Ledi, keep Loch Katrine on your left and the hills on your right. There's a fair few mountains between here and Appin, but you'll be all right as long as you go round them, not over. And go easy today — you'll hit the Crianlarich roundabout soon enough."

He smiled his crooked grin. "Soraidh slàn leat, Robbie, 's gach àit' an tèid thu."

Robbie shook his head. He recognized Gaelic, but he couldn't speak it.

"Farewell to you, wherever you go," Callum translated. With a wave of his hand, he turned and disappeared into the mist.

Chapter 17

They were barely off the ridge before Robbie almost ruined everything. He forgot Callum's warning about keeping his eyes open and hurried down the path, anxious to get out of the damp clinging mist. Turning a sharp corner, he stopped dead at the sight of a man stomping towards him, a ski pole in each hand. He stopped and stared at Robbie, taking in his rumpled clothes and grubby appearance.

"What are you doing up here on your own?"

Wordlessly, Robbie shook his head. The man's eyes swivelled round. Robbie saw the black tip of a stumpy tail disappear behind the rocks.

The man frowned. "Where are your folks?"

"In ... in the car park." There must be a car park somewhere nearby.

"Well, tell them to get those dogs off the hill right now! They're not allowed to roam free," snapped the man. "Don't you know this is sheep country?"

Robbie nodded. The man glared at him for a moment more before he shouldered his way past, forcing Robbie up against the rocks, and continued on his way. Robbie waited till the mist swallowed him up, then stepped off the path. It was going to be rough going from now on.

On this side of the mountain, there were no trees, only rough grass and bare rock. Robbie picked his way carefully, trying to avoid anything that looked too steep, but it was hard to work out where he was heading.

A stiff breeze sprang up, driving the mist away, and he stopped, breathless and sweating, to catch his breath. He had finally reached the lower slopes of Ben Ledi. From here, he noticed gratefully, the land dropped much more gently, down towards a valley that stretched far into the distance. The landscape glittered with silver ribbons. There was a lot of water down there. Which meant bog.

Off to the right he could see the road, busy with morning traffic, cars and lorries winding their way up and over the towering, snow-capped mountain at the other end of the valley. Robbie watched them wistfully. If he had been travelling on that road, then Appin would be no more than a few hours away.

He had been right about the car park. It was close to the road, at the end of a narrow track. He could see one or two people moving about down there, but from this distance, they were little more than coloured dots. Robbie was taller than most boys his age, and even with binoculars, he felt sure that no one would be able to tell he wasn't a grown-up. Thanks to their spotted coats, the cats were almost impossible to see against the background of bracken and mossy rock.

He put a hand up to his eyes and squinted over to the west at the gleaming surface of Loch Katrine. Callum had told him to use that as a guide, following the edge of the loch, past the foothills of the mountains until he found the road again. After that, he had to follow the road north to Bridge of Orchy. Once he got there, he planned to rely on his own inner sense of direction to lead him through Glen Etive and over the last of the mountains into Appin.

For the first time, he realized the true scale of the journey he planned to undertake ... and its risks. Apart from Callum, no one knew where he was. If he got hurt, or lost, he was on his own. He didn't have one of those expensive phones that allowed you to call for help no matter where you were. He looked down at the car park. There was probably a pay phone down there. It would be so easy to walk down there, make a call, and wait for someone to come.

Instead, he hefted the pack more firmly on to his shoulders and scrambled down the last of the slope. At the bottom, he turned his back to the road, striking out across the valley. He wasn't giving up. He was going home.

Early that afternoon, Robbie stopped beside a stream, at a small sandy cove where he was sheltered from view by an overhanging clump of earth. The cats were not particularly happy with the boggy terrain, but there had been no complaints. Baldur was no longer the fearful creature Robbie had walked beside on Sherrifmuir, flinching at every passing bird and cringing from every drop of water on his fur.

Robbie sat down and sighed with satisfaction, proud of the progress he had made so far. Apart from that one meeting with the man on the hill, he had kept well away from other people, safely negotiating a huge chunk of boggy, treacherous ground. But he had only just settled down and closed his eyes when his peace was shattered. His eyes flew open. Baldur was sending a message of excitement, delight and anticipation. The cats had found something to eat. And it wasn't a rabbit.

He scrambled up the bank and froze in horror at the sight of Baldur and Freya eagerly tearing into a limp, woolly body lying half in and half out the water. It looked abandoned, but Robbie felt sure that sooner or later, someone would come looking for it. If they saw teeth marks on the carcase, then the hunt would be on. And this time, it wouldn't be a tranquillizer dart. The people who owned the sheep would be armed with shotguns.

"Leave it alone!" He dashed across the spongy bank and slid down beside the cats, pulling and heaving at Baldur's solid body. But the cat shrugged him off like some annoying insect.

"You can't eat this," hissed Robbie. "It belongs to someone!"

Baldur didn't even bother to look up. Robbie scooped up a handful of pebbles and threw them at the cat. Baldur leaped up, yowling. They snarled into each other's faces.

After an eternal moment, Baldur dropped his eyes. Robbie stood with his chest heaving, fighting the blinding panic that still threatened to overwhelm him.

"You can't have it," he insisted, when he was finally able to speak. "Do you want to be caught?" He sent an image of a man with a gun like the one Gavin Moir had tried to use. "Eat rabbits! You can only eat rabbits."

At last, Baldur's awareness of Robbie's fear won out over his desire for food. Grudgingly, the cat turned and walked away. But Freya was a different matter. Robbie watched her nuzzling into the body, her muzzle red, purring thunderously until, suddenly, Baldur was back, darting in and out, nipping repeatedly at her hindquarters until she lost patience and chased after him. Baldur kept on going, drawing her further and further away from the stream.

Relieved that Baldur had managed to get Freya away from the dead body, Robbie hurried to retrieve his pack and set off after them.

Freya wasn't in the least bit happy about her lost meal. She kept turning her head to look behind her, but she didn't go back. She didn't want to lose contact with Baldur. It was like the story of the Golden Goose ... Baldur was stuck to Robbie, and Freya was stuck to Baldur.

But it wasn't the end of things as far as Baldur was concerned. He moved closer to Robbie, who plodded on between pools of stagnant water, fighting a sick feeling in his stomach as he tried to work out how much of that anger had been Baldur's and how much was his — and whether that made any difference anyway.

Sheep are not ours to take.

"No," said Robbie. "They belong to someone else." He waved an arm. "All this land belongs to someone. We're allowed to walk on it, but we'd get into real trouble if you went after the sheep."

There was a pause, then Baldur asked, *Where is my land?*

Robbie carried on walking. He didn't know what to say. He couldn't think of any answer that might make sense to the cat.

What is deer?

Robbie blinked. He had forgotten that Baldur had been in the cave when Callum talked about hunting. The picture of a stag standing on top of a hill, antlers raised, popped into Robbie's mind, and he shivered at Baldur's delight as he plucked the image from his head.

"There might be deer here," Robbie admitted grudgingly. In fact he was sure there were. "But you can't hunt here. I'll take you someplace safe."

Will there be deer at this other place?

"Yes," sighed Robbie. "There will be deer."

Satisfied, Baldur left Robbie to negotiate his way across the rough ground.

As the day wore on, he drew gradually closer to the mountain he had seen from Ben Ledi. Soon he was moving up again, on to higher ground. Callum had told him what it was called, but Robbie couldn't remember. He stared up at its snow-capped summit, glad that he didn't have to cross the top. Tomorrow, he would be dipping down again into the valley.

He finally called a halt early in the evening, choosing a wooded slope where a stand of trees offered shelter and a clear view of the distant road, which glittered now with a thousand lights. He would sleep here tonight and stay on, during the hours of daylight, until it was safe to cross the road. That would give the cats a chance to hunt. It should be reasonably safe. This was the time of year when the summer walkers — all but a hardy few — packed their gear away for the winter. And the skiers would still be waiting for what they called 'serious' snow. There wouldn't be many people about.

It was cold on the hillside now he was no longer moving. He drew up his knees and wrapped his arms around them, chewing a strip of dried meat, watching the car lights. People were hurrying home for the night.

Baldur lay down behind him and Robbie leaned back into the cat's solid body, relishing the warmth. A short while later, he was asleep. He woke once during the night, to find that Freya had joined the huddle. If it weren't for the rough ground beneath him, Robbie could almost have believed that he was snug at home in his own bed.

Chapter 18

The cats disappeared for most of the next day and Robbie made the most of his solitude. For the first time in days he was free to think his own thoughts and free from Callum's unpredictable behaviour.

He stayed in the woods until the sun was low in the sky, then set off towards the road, where he waited, crouched in the bushes until long after nightfall, watching while the traffic slowed to no more than a trickle. Only then did he hurry across the dark surface of the road with the cats close beside him, and then set out on the long, spooky walk through the night towards Tyndrum.

Unwilling to trust himself to the treacherous, boggy moorland, he kept as close to the road as he dared. But the ground was lumpy and uneven, so that he blundered along erratically, his feet twisting on unseen rocks, in constant danger of falling or wrenching his ankle.

The cats had no such problems and Robbie had to put up with Baldur constantly nibbling at his mind, curious to find out why his progress was so slow. When Baldur finally worked out that Robbie could see almost nothing, he arrived at his side, nudging him gently one way and another. Eventually Robbie took hold of the loose skin around the cat's neck and let himself be guided all the way through the endless darkness.

It was almost dawn and he was stumbling with weariness when he crossed the road leading down into Glen Orchy and set off across the moor, heading for a distant patch of woodland, where he finally found shelter beneath a wind-blown tree bent almost flat to the ground, its roots pointing up towards the sky. Robbie threw the plastic sheet over the top, crept into the hole, and closed his eyes.

He woke slowly, to the sound of rain dripping on the plastic sheet. The cats were nowhere in sight. They were probably out hunting. It had been a long night, and a hungry one. Robbie hoped Baldur had not found any deer. This close to the main road, it was still very much human territory.

Shivering in the damp air, he reached for his pack. There wasn't much left of the meat Callum had given him. He sat beneath his plastic roof, chewing the last of it, eyeing a huge, trumpet-shaped fungus growing from the trunk of a nearby tree. There was probably plenty to eat around here, if only he knew how to find it. But he knew it wasn't worth the risk. He didn't want to end up poisoning himself.

His meagre breakfast over, he packed up and set off, hoping his night walk had taken him far enough north to avoid Loch Etive. Thanks to the rain, he had no idea whether it was morning or afternoon, but he needed to get as far as he could before dark. The cats would find him when they were ready.

The wood ended abruptly on the shores of a loch dotted with a series of small islands. Robbie watched a train moving slowly northward on the other side of the loch. A vast flock of birds took off from one of the islands, wheeling and dipping across the sky, and he glanced around nervously. This must be a popular spot with birdwatchers. With their powerful binoculars, they could be watching him right now and he wouldn't know it.

He hurried away from the water, back into the shelter of the trees, where he soon discovered that he was right. This was not the deserted landscape it appeared to be. In a clearing deep in the woods he came across a little wooden house, hardly more than a shed. He knew what it was — a bothy, where anyone who needed shelter could find food and fuel for a fire.

Robbie looked at it longingly, but he didn't dare risk it. From a distance, he could pass for a short and extremely grubby adult, but close up it was obvious he was too young to be travelling alone. Somebody might turn up — or might even be there already.

Almost as though the thought had conjured him up, Robbie saw the door open, and a man stepped outside. Robbie faded back out of sight as the man yawned, scratched one armpit and looked around, bleary-eyed. He stayed where he was, motionless, while the man wandered round the back of the bothy to relieve himself and finally disappeared back indoors. Only then did Robbie move off, walking as swiftly as he could, careful not to make any noise.

He travelled on through moor and woodland, the land once more rising gradually higher. Soon he was scrambling over craggy outcrops and inching his way across slopes slippery with loose rock.

He made sure to avoid any paths that other people might be using. At least there was no need to worry about roads ... not until Glen Etive, and that was just a narrow single-track lane, with passing places.

The cats ranged widely, growing in confidence as the land grew wilder. Robbie would look up to see a pointed face peering at him from behind a rock and wave before he carried on. It was comforting to know he wasn't totally on his own.

From time to time he stopped to rest, his eyes travelling across the vast expanse of moor and rock, thinking about what Callum had told him. This might be human territory now, but once, these hills and mountains were covered in dense forest, home to wolves and wild boar, a place where solitary travellers moved through a world filled with danger.

"I would have been safe though," thought Robbie. "Safer than I am now." Without his tranquillizer gun, Gavin Moir would not dare to challenge the power of Freya and Baldur.

As evening approached, the rain dampened down to a soft drizzle then disappeared altogether, to be replaced by a breeze that chilled Robbie to the bone. He found a meagre shelter between two hanging rocks. The space was small, barely enough for a boy and two large cats, but at least it was dry.

He crawled inside as far as he could go, then pulled off his pack and took out the sheep's wool Callum had given him, then placed it carefully on the ground, surrounding it with a small heap of twigs. It was hard to do in the dark and he used quite a few matches before he managed to get it alight. With the small store of branches he had collected along the way, he built up the fire, sheltering it carefully from the breeze, adding twigs a few at a time until it was blazing brightly enough to survive on its own.

From outside came the rattle of falling pebbles and both cats squeezed themselves inside the narrow space to crouch beside him, their bodies forming a welcome barrier against the wind. Robbie lay down on the bare rock, his head pillowed on the mouldy backpack, and closed his eyes, trying to ignore the demands of his empty stomach.

His last thought before sleep overtook him was that tomorrow, if he was lucky, he would be in the hills beyond Glen Etive, crossing the last barrier between him and his goal.

Callum had told Robbie to go round the mountains, not up and over the top and the wide, rock-strewn corridor running between two towering slopes — that he found shortly after starting out the next morning — seemed to be exactly what he was looking for. But as he followed its meandering twist and turns, he realized that the rock walls were slowly coming together, until he was forcing his way through an increasingly narrow gap in the hillside.

He grinned in relief when he squeezed past a boulder and saw the passage opening out again, but instead of a clear vista down towards Glen Etive, he found himself staring up at a wall of stone. It was as tall as a two-storey house.

Robbie had two choices. Either he could retrace his steps and waste a couple of hours' progress, or he could climb. He studied the rock face, thinking hard. It was steep, almost vertical, but he could see plenty of hand and footholds. And he couldn't bear the thought of going back. It had taken him most of the morning to get this far. If he wanted to get to Glen Etive today, he had no choice. He frowned up at the overhanging rocks at the top, looking for the best place to aim for before starting the climb.

Making up his mind, he moved towards the foot of the wall, tightened the pack on his back and then began to pick his way up with total concentration, making sure every hand and foothold was secure before moving on to the next. He soon discovered that the wall was not as solid as it looked. Even the smallest of movements sent loose pebbles skittering down to the bottom.

Unlike Robbie, the cats moved up with surefooted grace, arriving at the top even before Robbie had managed to climb more than his own body height off the ground. Inch by inch, he crawled upward, freezing with dread every time a stone came away in his hand. He didn't look up or down, focusing only on the rock wall a few inches from his face. It felt as though he had been climbing for hours when his upraised hand banged painfully against an outcrop of rock and he realized he was almost there. He risked a quick glance up, to see Baldur peering down at him.

With a surge of relief, Robbie knew he was going to make it. Just a couple more steps and then he would be able to drag himself up to the top. He lifted one foot and placed it carefully on the next stone, realizing his mistake only when the stone shifted and tilted, throwing him sideways.

His hands stung as he slapped them against the rock, desperately seeking anything that might halt his downward slide. Hanging on by his fingertips, he hugged the rock face, afraid to move until his body stopped shaking and his heart calmed down. But he knew that time was running out. He had to find a firmer foothold before his fingers lost their fragile grip.

But though his brain was sending the message, his body was frozen with fear and he clung on while sweat trickled down his forehead, stinging his eyes. He could do nothing about it. He was afraid even to blink.

Now, when it was far too late, he saw how one wrong decision had led to another; an inevitable progression towards this moment when he would die, alone, in the mountains, with no one to help, even if he survived the fall.

It took a monumental effort for him to shift his weight on to one foot and began to lift the other, looking for something more stable. But nothing happened. His foot stayed where it was. With dawning horror, Robbie realized that his boot was jammed. And he couldn't lever it free without losing his balance. He was stuck! Any moment now, his hands would lose their grip and he would fall. At the very least, he would break his ankle. And if the stones that imprisoned him gave way, then he would tumble headfirst all the way down to the rocks below.

He plastered his cheek against the rough stone while his brain tried to reassure him that this wasn't real. It couldn't be. Soon, he would wake up to find it was nothing more than a bad dream. A loose pebble rattled past, hitting him painfully on the ear and he heard an odd, clicking sound. By the time he realized that the noise was the sound of claws on stone, Baldur was already below him, his teeth gripping Robbie's boot.

Baldur shook the boot while Robbie made a monumental effort to force his fear and panic to the back of his mind. He could not afford to distract the cat. The boot came free just as his numb fingers slipped off the rock face. Baldur leaped past him and he reached out frantically, grabbing hold of the cat's tail using it as a rope to haul himself up and over the top, where he lay gasping for breath, his feet still dangling over empty space.

Eventually he dragged himself on to his hands and knees, then up on his feet. He stared at the wide expanse of purple moorland unrolling all the way down to Glen Etive. The cats were looking at him, both wearing the same puzzled expression, as though they couldn't believe he had made such a disaster of a simple climb.

"Sorry about your tail," he said. Hesitantly, he reached over and ran his hand across the soft fur on Baldur's head. "I think maybe you saved my life."

As you saved mine, Baldur sent back.

Chapter 19

Robbie walked out of the bleak desolation of the hills, back into a world where the sun still warmed the rocks and the mild breeze held no hint of the bitter winter winds yet to come. Callum had been wrong about the midges. There were still a few left, but luckily the dense black clouds of the summer were gone, leaving nothing more than a minor nuisance.

He sat down beside a little wooden bridge and pulled off his boots. His ankle was a little swollen, but apart from that, and an aching arm where he had twisted round to grab hold of Baldur, he was surprisingly intact.

Rejecting the bridge, Freya picked her way across the rocks to the other side of the river and set off to investigate the trees and bushes. Baldur followed her only as far as the middle of the stream, where he sat down on a sun-warmed stone, watching intently as the water bubbled and foamed its way between the rocks. Robbie stared longingly at the sparkling water. His whole body itched and his hair was stiff and sticky. He felt horribly dirty.

Not giving himself time to think, he stripped off his clothes, clambered up on the rocks and slid down, almost up to his waist, into the water. He gasped in shock as he felt the river's cold embrace. The day might be sunny, but the river water was close to freezing. He changed his mind. There was no way he wanted to lower himself any further.

He looked up at Baldur. The cat blinked lazily and stretched out across the rock, clearly enjoying the warmth of the sun. Seized by sudden mad impulse, Robbie brought the flat of his hand hard down on the surface of the water, sending an icy wave right up and over the cat.

Baldur leaped to his feet, scrabbling for balance on the damp rocks. He didn't look very dignified any more, not with those drooping whiskers and his fur standing up in spikes all over his head.

Robbie laughed aloud at the cat's outraged expression and brought his hand down again. It was a mistake. Baldur took off in a springing leap, aiming straight for him. He barely had time to register the full awfulness of what was about to happen before the cat landed right on top of him.

His feet slipped on the slimy rocks and he fell backwards in utter panic. The icy water drove all the air from his lungs and he turned frantically, fighting his way back to the surface.

Spluttering and gasping, he glared at Baldur, who was belly-deep in the middle of the stream, looking at him with deep amusement.

"I thought cats didn't like to get their fur wet." His teeth chattered so hard he could barely get the words out. He staggered towards the bank, pulling on his clothes without waiting till he dried off. On the other side of the stream, Baldur was licking his fur back into proper shape.

"I suppose I deserved that," Robbie said, then he grinned. "But it was worth it."

He sat down and lifted his face to the sun, relishing its warmth on his tingling skin. There was no point in thinking about food. Everything Callum had given him was gone. The cats might be willing to share what they caught, but he shrank from the prospect of learning how to skin and gut the body of some small creature only recently dead.

Baldur yawned, then disappeared into the undergrowth after Freya. Robbie leaned back against a rock and closed his eyes. Moments later, the sound of wheels on gravel warned him that he was no longer alone. He sat up and peered through the trees just in time to see a van draw up on the small turn-off next to the road.

The back opened and he watched a young man jump out, followed by three more people. As they began to unload backpacks and boots, the side door opened and a girl stepped down from the driver's seat.

"We'll eat first," she called over her shoulder. "I'm starving. And I'm not doing any more climbing till I've had my lunch."

She stretched both arms over her head, walked slowly down to the water and collapsed face first on to the grass, taking no notice of the chorus of derisive shouts from the crowd unloading the van.

Robbie stood up. He didn't want to look as though he was skulking in the bushes. The girl looked at him in surprise.

"Hi, there," she said brightly. "Where did you come from?"

She glanced up and down the road, obviously wondering how he had got there. It was a long way to the nearest house and Robbie knew there was no way she would believe he was part of a walking party.

"I come here for the fishing," he improvised. "My Dad dropped me off. He's picking me up later."

"Aha!" she said. "A local!"

Robbie nodded.

"So where's your fishing gear?"

He gestured vaguely upstream. "Over there. I fancied a walk. It's nice and peaceful here."

Her eyes narrowed and she looked at him more closely. But then she shrugged, clearly losing interest. "You're right," she said, and grinned. "It must have been very peaceful before we turned up."

Robbie sat back down as the rest of the group made their way down to the water. One of them tossed a carrier bag at the girl. She opened it and examined its contents with a critical frown before she looked up to see Robbie watching her.

"Eaten your lunch already, have you?"

Robbie gave a laugh that sounded false even to him. "Hours ago," he said.

"Want some?" She reached over and put something in his hand.

Robbie looked down at the sandwich. It contained a thick slab of cheese, topped with slices of tomato. Using every ounce of self-control he possessed, he raised it slowly to his mouth and took a single bite instead of cramming the whole thing in at once.

"Don't suppose you want any of this though." She waved a beer can in his direction.

"No thanks." He sat down, forcing himself to chew slowly and steadily as the laughter and chat bounced from one member of the group to another.

At last they were ready to move on and Robbie watched, disappointed, as they carefully deposited the remains of their picnic in the back of the van before they set off across the bridge lugging helmets, ropes, spiked boots and various other bits of equipment.

One of them turned to another. Making no effort to lower his voice, he said, "Do you think all the locals sleep in their clothes?"

Some of them giggled, others ordered him to shush. Robbie watched them disappear into the trees, hating their easy companionship, their sleek, well-fed looks and shiny clean faces. With a sudden burst of longing, he pulled out his phone. He stared at it for a long time. But what was the use of a phone when you had no one to call?

With a sudden impulsive gesture, he lifted his arm and threw it as far as he could. Then he bent to pull on his boots and socks. Half the day was gone, but he felt sure he could still cover a fair distance before night. He would start as soon as the happy gang were far enough ahead so he could keep out of their way.

The cats emerged from the undergrowth as he crossed the river, to make his way along the marked path. When it swung to the right, heading uphill, he struck off across the side of the slope, making sure he was well away from the track before he began to move higher, up through the trees and back into rough moorland.

No more mistakes, he told himself firmly. There would be no more short cuts ... and definitely no more cliffs.

Chapter 20

Thanks to the internal compass that had guided him all the way from the woodland near Bridge of Orchy, Robbie knew where he was going, but that didn't make it any easier to follow Callum's advice and avoid the higher peaks. Somehow, every path he chose took him a little bit further up. This was not one single mountain, but several, their massive peaks rearing up into the sky between him and his goal.

According to Callum, it was possible to follow the tracks that the Appin farmers once used to bring their cows to market. The trouble was, without a map, Robbie couldn't tell where they were. It was almost impossible to tell the difference between a sheep track and the remains of some ancient cattle route.

He wound his way upwards, trying to find a route through the valleys, backtracking whenever a promising route ended in a steep downward scramble. Every so often he would pass a gap in the rocks, but he had learned his lesson and rejected their tempting invitation, recognising them for the traps they were.

With his hood pulled up to protect him from the thin, biting wind, he toiled upward, his unease growing as the air grew colder. The old cattle drovers had spent years learning how to read the mountains, but Robbie didn't have their skill. At this height, each hill blended into the other, making it hard for him to tell whether he was moving forward at all or just walking aimlessly up and down.

He crossed one windswept ridge, then another, envying the cats their effortless progress. Already, one massive peak was behind him. Sunlight glittered on frost, reflecting light all around. Robbie knew the afternoon was almost over. It was obvious that he wasn't going to make it over these mountains before nightfall. Very soon now, he would have to find a place to camp.

Beyond the ridge was a vast, open plateau, with little to offer in the way of shelter. Baldur and Freya trotted confidently forward across the icy surface, while Robbie followed more cautiously, unwilling to risk another fall, not even on level ground.

Robbie stopped. Clouds were gathering overhead. He lifted his head and sniffed the air. Beside him, Freya did the same. Baldur looked from one to the other. He could smell it too, but he had no idea what it was.

"Snow," said Robbie. "Snow is coming."

There was no point now in regretting his decision to cross the plateau. Choosing caution over speed, he rejected the impulse to try and make it to the other side before the snow came. Instead, he stopped in the lee of the biggest boulder he could find and began to construct a makeshift tent, anchoring the plastic sheet with piles of loose rock. As he crawled inside, the first white flakes were already drifting out of the sky,

He opened his pack. His hood, together with the musty-smelling Black Watch cap, would keep his head from freezing. He twisted about, wriggling into his extra trousers and sweatshirt, then he pulled out the strips of rabbit fur, weaving them in and out of his fingers and across his palms to create a pair of makeshift mittens. When the cats crawled inside to join him, he laid his head on the pack and curled up into a ball between them.

Outside the wind rose, whipping against the plastic sheet, sending gusts of snow piling up around them. No doubt by now, the jolly climbers were snug in their all-weather tent, swapping food and drink and stories. Robbie sighed and tucked his hands into his armpits. Huddled here on the cold, hard ground with only the cats for company, it was going to be a long, lonely night.

Not lonely, Baldur's thought came slow and drowsy. *Not lonely any more.*

When Robbie finally managed to fight his way free of the snow-covered plastic, he emerged into a white and silent world. Snow lay thick on the ground, drifts of it piled up against the side of the plastic sheet. He lifted his feet, trying to stamp some warmth back into his frozen toes. Yesterday's brilliant blue sky was no more than a memory. He frowned up at the dirty grey clouds. There was more snow to come. A lot more. He had to dismantle his makeshift camp and move on as fast as he could.

He squinted into the distance, at the grey-on-grey outline of two mountain peaks. Somewhere between those two hills there had to be a way down below the snowline. He turned away and began to tug the plastic free of its blanket of snow.

There was no point in thinking about what might happen if he couldn't find it.

Freya set off at her usual smooth pace but Baldur, unhappy with the alien nature of this smooth white surface, soon outdistanced her, lifting each foot as soon as it hit the ground. It would have been comical at any other time, but Robbie's urgent need to get off the mountain left no room for laughter. As he followed in Baldur's wake, the wind rose and snow began to fall again, softly at first, but with increasing violence, until it was whipping against him in blinding gusts.

A wall of stone suddenly materialized in front of him. He turned to follow it, desperately seeking a break in the rock. At last his outstretched hand met empty air and he stumbled out of the driving snow, the cats tumbling into the gap alongside him.

The crack led downhill, but Robbie's relief soon evaporated when what started as a sharp downward climb grew even steeper, until he was descending an almost vertical chimney. The wind howled through the narrow space, and scrabbling to hold on with both fingers and toes, he was unable to tell whether he was placing his feet on solid ground or merely a thin crust of ice and snow.

Robbie clung on desperately. Baldur's thoughts intruded into his mind, urging him to find someplace to wait out the storm, but Robbie pushed them away. There was nowhere to stop.

At last, the inevitable happened. A violent gust of wind knocked him sideways and he lost his grip, tumbling down the chimney onto a drift of snow and rolling head over heels until he fetched up against a jumble of rocks. A moment later, Baldur was at his side, licking his face and his hands; any part of him he could reach. Robbie rolled back against the snow-covered rock. He was too tired and too cold to get on his feet. A delicious warmth began to spread through his body and he gave himself up to it willingly. It was too hard. He couldn't go any further.

From the corner of his eyes, he saw something move against the white background. Puzzled, he shifted his head to follow it. Then he lurched to his feet. It was almost impossible to believe, but there was someone out there, only a short distance away.

Robbie stumbled forward, waving his hands. He knew he had to let them know he was here, but instead of a yell, all he could manage was a faint croak. The dark shape stopped and Robbie slithered to a halt, his harsh cries for help dying in his throat. He didn't need Freya's sudden intense interest to understand his mistake.

She crouched low to the ground and began to slide forward, one slow step at a time. Robbie fell back down in the snow as Baldur appeared beside him.

There's your deer. He turned to look at the cat. *You got your wish.*

You stay, I stay. Baldur was not going to leave him.

Robbie struggled to sit up. Go, he insisted. *I just need to rest for a while. I'll be fine.*

Baldur's head swung slowly from Robbie to the deer and back again. Robbie clung to the lie as he felt Baldur trying to push his way into his mind. It took a tremendous effort to struggle back on to his feet but somehow he managed it. Just a little bit further, he promised himself, just far enough to convince Baldur he didn't need any help and then, at last, he could lie down and give himself up to the sleep that would finally bring an end to cold and hunger and the constant struggle through this desolate white wilderness.

Robbie forced himself to walk a few steps and at last, with one final look, Baldur slipped away. But he only managed a few faltering steps before his legs collapsed beneath him and he was falling again, tumbling uncontrollably down the slope, not knowing or caring what might be waiting for him at the bottom. For the last time, he opened his eyes.

He blinked and reached up a frozen hand to rub snow from his eyelashes. It couldn't be ... but it was! A wooden ski lodge, tucked neatly into the lee of the hill. With a monumental effort, Robbie struggled upright and staggered across the slope, still half convinced it was a dream brought on by cold and exhaustion. Not until his groping fingers met the solid wooden door did he truly understand it wasn't his imagination. It was real. And it was locked.

Chapter 21

Weeping with frustration, Robbie pounded on the door until it finally penetrated his brain that he knew where the key might be. All the holiday houses did it up here. He fell to his knees, scrabbled in the snow until he unearthed a rubber mat. The key was underneath.

It took forever for his clumsy fingers to get the key in the lock, but at last there was a faint click and the door opened. The wind snatched at him, unwilling to let him go, as he stumbled inside, knocking over a pile of ski equipment in his hurry to reach the electricity box. He pulled it open and threw the trip switch. As the radiators bubbled into life, he turned and saw Baldur in the doorway, staring at Robbie with unblinking eyes.

"It's all r-right," he stuttered, feeling his frozen body start to shake as it came slowly back to life. "I'll be all right now."

Baldur looked at Robbie for a long moment. His emerald eyes gleamed. Then he turned away, heading back into the wind and snow.

Robbie shut the door, shrugged off his pack and wobbled his way into one of the bedrooms, where he grabbed a duvet and brought it back across the hall into the living room. He turned the electric fire full on, then dragged off his wet clothes and fell on to the duvet, rolling himself inside, gritting his teeth against the pain as his numb fingers and toes came slowly back to life. When at last the tingling stopped, he lay slumped on the rug in front of the fire, finally giving in to the overwhelming urge for sleep.

When he finally struggled back to consciousness, Robbie had no idea if it was still the same day or whether he had slept right round the clock. He stood up and wandered through to the kitchen, dragging the duvet along behind him like a great fleecy cloak. He peered out the window at dirty grey daylight. The wind had dropped, but the snow was still falling.

He remembered the pile of skis at the front door. There was plenty of snow out there now. He had lost track of time days ago, but if it was the weekend, then there was every chance that the owners of the chalet might turn up. He turned away from the window, knowing that it was pointless to worry. He had no choice. Without food and rest he couldn't carry on. The owners of the chalet would know the mountain code. They could not deny him food and shelter. And there was no point in worrying about what they would think of a boy travelling on his own.

A shiver ran down his back at the thought of how lucky he had been. Without the cats, he would be just one more name on the list of those who died in the mountains each year. If he hadn't seen the deer, he would still be out there, curled up in the snow. How long, he wondered, would Baldur have kept the vigil beside his frozen body before he finally gave up?

From somewhere nearby, he picked up a fleeting impression of well-fed satisfaction. It was a grisly reminder that what had been lucky for him was disastrous for another living creature. Robbie shuddered. He was used to food that came neatly packaged from the supermarket shelves, pre-cooked instant dinners that bore no resemblance to anything that might once have been alive. For the first time he understood the savage reality of hunter and prey.

But there was nothing he could do now for the deer. And he was very, very hungry. Turning from the window, he pulled open a cupboard. His mouth watered in anticipation as he grabbed a can of beans, pulled off the lid and raised it to his lips. Then he hesitated. After a long moment, he put the can down. He wasn't an animal. He would do this properly.

He fetched his clothes from the living room and stuffed them into the washing machine, then he padded down the hall to the bathroom, still dragging the duvet along behind him. After a blissful half hour soaking his aching muscles in the bath, he allowed himself back into the kitchen. It was definitely dinner time now.

While day faded into night, Robbie ate one packet of super noodles, then another. He followed that up with a tin of rice pudding and then, after a moment's thought, he finished off the beans as well. They would just go dry if he left them. His stomach bulging, he put his clothes into the tumble dryer, turned it on and then stretched out on the sofa with the duvet tucked round him to sleep again.

Robbie shouldered his pack, lifted the key and took one last look around. The duvet was back where it belonged, the dishes washed and neatly stacked beside the sink. Baldur — and presumably Freya — were waiting outside. They, too, had fed well.

He placed a grubby ten-pound note on the kitchen counter. Thanks to Callum, he didn't have to feel like a thief. Then he walked through the living room into the hall, turned off the electricity and opened the door to the outside world.

The sky was clear, the air crisp and dry. Although the cats must have left plenty evidence of their presence, already the wind was blowing powdered snow over their tracks. By the time winter was over, the deer would be no more than a pile of scattered bones.

Far in the distance, he could see the Isle of Mull. The mountains were behind him now. Not far below, a narrow road wound its way down the hill to where the hills and valleys of Appin stretched all the way to the sea. High above him, a buzzard hung in the sky. Baldur lifted his head to stare up at it, one predator watching another. It was hard to believe the lynx was the same timid creature who had been so terrified by the world outside his cage.

Robbie stepped out briskly, his boots crunching on the snow. Very soon, he was walking on the tarmac surface of the road. An hour or so later, he reached the tree line and struck off from the road into the woods. His hair was neatly combed, he was clean, well rested and well fed, just an ordinary boy out on a quiet stroll. No one would guess he was walking through unknown country, following the thread that led him home.

But the land soon grew familiar. He passed the tumbledown remains of an old croft house, its roof long gone, and emerged from the trees at a dilapidated stone bridge, where the hill split in two and a waterfall plunged steeply down over mossy, fern-covered rocks. People must have farmed here once, but not any more. The forest had reclaimed the land. He stood on the slippery green cobbles of the bridge looking down at the pool far below, where the waterfall turned back into a tumbling stream. He frowned thoughtfully.

"I've been here before," he said.

Baldur looked up at him.

"I came with my grandmother when I was small." Robbie pointed to the waterfall. "There's a cave in there, behind the water. The Cave of the Skulls. They found bones there, from people who lived a long time ago. Ancient people."

He frowned in concentration as a distant memory surfaced. They came here and she let him climb a little way up the hill until he could see the dark shadow of the cave behind the water, but she wouldn't let him go inside. Afterwards, they went somewhere else for ice cream before they went home. He remembered lying in bed that night, listening to the sound of raised voices from the living room, wishing he could go through to join the grown-ups. But he couldn't. His father and his grandmother were arguing. About him? Maybe, thought Robbie, his grandmother had wanted him to know the truth. Maybe that was why she had brought him here.

He looked around. "They must have liked this place," he said. "Plenty to eat in the forest, fish from the river, a sheer cliff at your back and an open view ahead — you can see anyone coming from a long way off."

Baldur gave the mental equivalent of a shrug. Those ancient people held no interest for him.

"Not much further," Robbie said, as he walked forward on to the road beyond the bridge.

Two hours later, he stood on a low hill looking down at the little house standing in an open space among the trees. It was hard to believe it was real. His journey was finally over. He was home.

Taking a deep breath, he picked his way slowly down the hill with Baldur, as always, by his side. He dragged open the lopsided garden gate, fetched the key from the doorstep and then paused to look behind him. Though he couldn't see her, he knew Freya was still on the hill. The man-made shelter below held no interest for her.

Robbie stepped inside and stopped dead at the sight of a banked up fire glowing in the stove and a fresh plate of sandwiches on the kitchen table.

Chapter 22

He moved closer and bent to look at the note on the table. *Gone for a walk. Back soon.* Robbie scowled down at the familiar handwriting. Then he moved back beside Baldur and shut the door firmly. Ignoring the food on the table, he marched across to the old wooden chair beside the stove and sat down.

"We're staying." This was his place. No one was going to take it from him ... or *him* from it.

Slightly puzzled, Baldur crossed the room and flopped down in front of the stove with his head on his paws.

Hardly any time passed before Robbie heard the creak of the gate. Then the door flew open. Michael Bruce stood in the doorway, panting for breath.

"I saw you on the hill," he gasped. "I thought maybe I was imagining it, but I wasn't. You're here, aren't you?" His eyes were shining. "You're really here." He looked at the food on the table, then back at Robbie. "I thought you would be hungry," he said. "I've left you something every day, just in case."

Robbie stood up. "This is my house," he said coldly. "Not yours."

Baldur growled. Michael glanced at the cat in surprise as though he'd only just noticed his presence.

"Oh, Robbie," he said, his voice filled with sadness. "I'm so sorry. I've made such a mess of it all. I thought I could take care of everything. But I got it wrong. I got it so wrong." He ran his fingers through his hair and shook his head. "All I've been hanging on to is the thought that you would come here."

"You lied to me," said Robbie. "All my life you've been lying to me."

Michael took a step forward and stopped as Baldur growled again. "No more lies," he said quietly. "I promise. No more lies." His eyes softened. "There are so many things I've wanted to tell you."

He reached into a pocket and pulled out a photograph, holding it in his outstretched hand. Robbie made no move to take it. But he couldn't help looking. The photograph was old and crumpled, as though someone had kept it for a very long time. But Robbie had never seen it before.

A thin, dark-haired woman lay propped up on a sofa — the sofa in the living room next door. She was looking down at the child in her arms, but the baby was looking straight into the eye of the camera.

"I remember," said Robbie, his voice soft with wonder. "I remember." It was nothing more than a sense of comfort and warmth, a smell, teasing the edges of his mind, but it was there.

"I watched her with you," his father said. "I came up here every chance I got. Do you see how her eyes smiled when I put you in her arms?" His voice wobbled and his eyes filled with tears. "How could I regret what she did? And she was right to do it. Because when she was gone, I still had you."

"You kept it a secret from me." Robbie's voice hardened again.

His father dropped his hand, still holding the photograph. "You were just a little boy, Robbie. I couldn't risk it. If you let something slip and they found out at the Institute, I thought they would take you away from me."

Michael looked at him longingly, but Robbie stayed where he was. This was a man who had put his career above everything, even above his son.

"Your mum always wanted children ... but then she got sick, and it was too late."

He didn't notice the cat lift his head in sudden interest. He had no idea he was talking to anyone other than his son. But Robbie knew that Baldur wanted the truth just as much as he did.

Michael rubbed a hand over his eyes. "She managed to persuade Stella to carry a baby for her. She took her own eggs, removed the damaged genes and replaced them with what she was working on ... the Hox genes. Stella didn't know about that. Neither did I."

"She said you were a coward," said Robbie. It was a struggle to keep his voice steady, to hide the storm of emotions brought on by the sight of his father stumbling through old secrets, with the tears running down his face. "She said you'd always been a coward."

Michael nodded, his face sombre. "Stella's right. I was frightened. I couldn't bear the thought of what might happen to your mum if anyone found out. And then, later ..." his eyes dwelt on Robbie for a long moment. "I couldn't bear the thought of losing you. There was nothing I could do about the published work, but I got rid of everything else. I got Joe and Stella to agree that we had to keep quiet. And it worked. But then Moir arrived. He persuaded Joe to carry on the research that your mum had started. Baldur was Joe's proof that he could duplicate her work."

Robbie nodded. He remembered the eager, greedy look on Joe's face when he talked about Baldur.

"I had to tell Moir about you," said Michael. "But it didn't make any difference. He wouldn't listen." His voice hardened. "And then I found out I hadn't got rid of everything after all. There was human DNA as well as the Hox gene in the samples Joe was using."

"Stella Loomis told me that," said Robbie. "She said mum couldn't make it work with just the human gene, so she linked it to the Hox gene because she had managed to insert that before."

Michael nodded. For the first time he looked directly at Baldur. "That cat carries the same Hox gene as you do ... and a very small piece of human DNA as well."

Robbie stared at his father. "But he's still a cat, isn't he?"

In spite of everything, it felt good to hear his father laugh. "Of course he's still a cat, Robbie! You're still a human!"

"Where did the extra human DNA come from?"

Michael smiled. "From me, Robbie. It came from me."

"So a piece of your DNA is floating around inside Baldur?" This time it was Robbie's turn to laugh. "Hox genes change the way things grow, don't they?" he asked, feeling his way towards an understanding of how the strange link between him and Baldur had come about.

"Yes," said Michael. "But Jane never found any observable difference with the animals she worked on."

Maybe she hadn't, thought Robbie, but it had certainly made a difference to him. He looked down at Baldur, who rose to his feet and butted Robbie with his head before he looked up, his green eyes filled with new understanding.

We are new. And we are the same.

Baldur was right. The two extra pieces of DNA they shared had created something that had never existed before.

Robbie smiled nervously at his father. He still had one more question. The one he had resolutely refused to allow into his head ever since this began. "Are you ..." he swallowed and tried again. "Are you really my father?"

Michael looked at him with love and longing. "Oh, Robbie, of course I'm your father. Look at us ... we're the same shape, the same hair ... we've even got the same beaky nose."

"But there's more in me than just you and Mum," Robbie said uncertainly. "There's the Hox gene."

His father shrugged. "I've always known that. It never made any difference to me. Not since the first time I picked you up. You're my son. Something rare, and special, but still my son." He tilted his head and looked at him with a puzzled frown. "Robbie, you must know this was never about saving my job. I would have left long ago if I hadn't been afraid that someone would find out. All I ever wanted to do was to keep you safe."

He moved forward in a sudden rush, wrapping his arms around Robbie.

"I thought I'd lost you for ever."

His father hugged him so hard that Robbie felt his bones creak. And at last, the frozen lump of grief and anger he had carried inside for so long melted from his heart.

Chapter 23

To Robbie, it felt as though time was running backwards. Free at last from the need to guard his tongue, Michael talked endlessly of Robbie's birth, his early childhood and the mother he could barely remember, who hadn't died when Robbie was born, but had lived long enough to hear his first words and see him take his first, faltering steps. Robbie now knew why the cottage felt so much like home. He had lived here, hidden from the world, until he was almost two years old.

Baldur spent his days outside, sometimes with Robbie and Michael, more often joining Freya on her rambling explorations of her new kingdom. She still refused to come in the house. She had seemed happy enough with the cave, but maybe the cottage reminded her too much of the animal house. But Baldur appeared at the door every evening, ready for the warmth of the fire and Robbie's company. He curled at his feet like an overgrown house cat, his heavy-duty purr a constant background to the conversations that went on far into the night.

"I took samples when Baldur was born," said Michael. "That's when I found out I hadn't got rid of everything. I thought it would be enough to tell Gavin that you shared the Hox gene with Baldur, but he wasn't interested."

Robbie nodded. That must have been the argument he overheard.

"We never got to that meeting in Edinburgh, Robbie. We were on our way when I told him that

Baldur's DNA included a human gene. Gavin knew that any scientist looking at samples would find that out ... that's when he decided he had to get rid of Baldur and start again. We were already on our way back to Duncraig when Joe phoned to say you had run off with the cats."

Michael rubbed a hand across his face and sighed. "I waited for two weeks," he said. "I told the school you had flu. Ally phoned a couple of times but I just said you were sleeping. But you never came home." He looked into the fire for a moment and then at Robbie, his eyes deep and shadowy. "Then I thought about this place. I couldn't stay in Duncraig anyway. It's half term. Ally would have come looking for you."

Robbie shook his head, thinking how odd it was that something so important as the half term break had no meaning for him any more. "What day is it?"

"It's Thursday," said his Dad. He reached out and ruffled Robbie's hair, reassuring himself that Robbie was really there. "Only three weeks since I lost you ... but it feels like a lifetime." He looked at his son with a puzzled frown. "How did you do it Robbie? You just seemed to disappear off the face of the earth."

So Robbie told him, starting from the very beginning. As he described his first night on Sherrifmuir with only the cats for company, Robbie saw the shadows deepen on his father's face. He wasn't an old man, but the strain of the last few weeks had etched new lines across his forehead. Robbie skimmed over his near disaster on the rocks and decided not to mention how close he had come to falling asleep forever on the snow-covered mountains.

"I should have told Joe everything," said Michael. "If I had, then he would never have let you anywhere near Baldur."

Baldur's ear twitched. Michael never seemed to notice that the cat responded to what he said, but that was another thing Robbie decided to keep to himself. It was Baldur's secret, not his. Sometimes, he found himself watching the cat, wondering just how different he really was, but it didn't really matter very much. Baldur was Baldur.

It was a peaceful time, but after a few days Robbie found himself growing anxious. He could tell that his father still hoped to work out a reasonable solution with Gavin Moir and Joe. But Robbie didn't. Not after that terrifying encounter at the roadside.

"Gavin Moir wants to get rid of Baldur," he said to his father. "And what is he planning to do about me?"

Michael's smile was reassuring. "There's nothing he can do to you, son."

But Robbie wasn't so sure.

"Let him come," said his father. "I'll be here. I've got no reason to go anywhere." He reached out and ruffled Robbie's hair. "I've got no reason to go back."

"What about the cats?"

"They're not going back either," said Michael firmly. "Your mum used to say that humans had to learn to share. I think she was right."

Robbie looked down as Baldur's rumbling purr grew momentarily louder. "I'm not going to hide."

"I'm not asking you to," said Michael. "Not any more. Believe me, Robbie, I know how it feels to spend your whole life looking over your shoulder."

"We have to speak to them, then," said Robbie. "But not here. I don't want them to come here. We'll find somewhere else. Somewhere not too far away." Robbie couldn't face any more travelling. And he didn't want to leave Appin.

His father nodded. "You don't have to do this alone, Robbie. Not any more. I think you've done enough. I'll talk to Moir."

Robbie looked doubtfully at his father. It felt good to have him here beside him, but he didn't think he'd been much help so far.

But Michael wasn't stupid. He knew what Robbie was thinking.

"I've done a lot of things wrong, Robbie, but I got you this far, son."

Robbie flushed. "I know, Dad," he said.

We hunt together.

Robbie shivered at the underlying savagery in Baldur's head, but he knew the cat was right. It was his fight too. He watched his father struggle with the urge to take charge. It wasn't easy to change the habit of a lifetime. But Michael had learned that Robbie was no longer the boy he had been.

"I won't run any more," he said. "There are things I need to say to Joe and Gavin Moir. And I can speak for myself. Keeping secrets works both ways, Dad."

His father looked at him in dawning understanding and Robbie grinned.

"The only way Moir can get away with this is because you don't want anyone to find out about me. But if the truth comes out, then they will never be able to work on the Hox genes again. If they want me to keep quiet, then they'll have to let Baldur — and Freya — alone."

Robbie sat on the low parapet of the mossy old bridge watching a car crawl up the hill towards him. He knew who was in the car. He also knew who was in the Land Rover behind it. He swung one leg, tapping his heel against the stone. The falling water drowned out any other sound, but he didn't need ears to know that Baldur was nearby. And if Baldur was there, then so was Freya.

The car drew to a halt. Robbie saw Michael climb out and stand beside the car, waiting for Joe and Gavin Moir to join him. He waved a reassuring hand at Robbie as the two men emerged from the Land Rover. Michael pointed to Robbie and then all three walked together on to the bridge. Robbie swallowed, dry-mouthed. He was glad to be sitting down. He didn't want Moir to see how his body trembled with tension.

"Hallo, Robbie." Moir smiled. "I'm glad you finally decided to be sensible." His eyes flicked past him. Robbie looked back to see both cats sitting side by side, well away from the haze of spray that hung around the tumbling water.

"I'm not ..." Robbie cleared his throat and started again. "I didn't come here to let you take the cats."

Behind Moir, Robbie saw his father give an encouraging smile. Joe said nothing. He just stared at him, chewing furiously.

Moir cocked his head. "Is that so?"

A spurt of anger dampened Robbie's fear and he stood up, determined to wipe that superior smile off Moir's face.

"You think you can keep me quiet because I don't want anyone to know about me." He took a deep breath. "But Dad and I have talked. What happens to me doesn't matter. It's Baldur that matters. You have to leave the cats alone."

"Nothing's been published yet." Michael intervened. "All you have to do is let people know the cats have died. You can begin again." To Joe, he said bitterly, "I didn't know you were using Jane's private samples."

"You didn't tell me they might be carrying human DNA," replied Joe.

Robbie shivered. Was that what Joe thought? That Robbie and Baldur were nothing more than an experiment gone wrong?

Moir didn't even bother to look in the cats' direction. It was Robbie he wanted. He walked forward until he was standing right in front of him.

"You don't understand, do you?" His voice was pitched low, so that only Robbie could hear. "You're wrong, Robbie. You do matter. You matter very much indeed. You're the problem. Not Baldur. Because you don't know what you are."

"I know *who* I am, if that's what you mean." Robbie tried to keep his voice firm even though his heart quaked at the determination he saw in

Moir's eyes. "Not something old. Something new. So is Baldur."

Joe stopped chewing. "Maybe Robbie's right, Gavin," he said. "Do we really have the right to say they shouldn't be here? We're all animals after all."

Moir went on as though Joe hadn't spoken. "You see, Robbie, I realized something when you took off with Baldur. It was the cat we wanted then, of course. Because we couldn't take the risk of letting his altered genes loose in the wild."

He stepped a little closer and Robbie forced himself not to flinch.

"I'm a scientist, Robbie," Moir said. "Science is about unravelling puzzles. I'm sure you know that. But we are also responsible for making sure we do no damage. Your mother committed a crime, Robbie. She let something loose in you." He jabbed Robbie with his finger. "And it has to be stopped."

"But I'm here now," said Robbie. "So there's not much you can do about it, is there?"

Moir laughed. "Don't be childish, Robbie." His good humour evaporated as quickly as it had appeared. "But that's what you are, isn't it? A child. A very dangerous child. We can't have you loose in the human gene pool."

"Leave him alone!" Michael's voice was drowned out by a sudden surge of anger from Baldur.

Robbie flinched.

Moir eyes flashed contempt. But he couldn't feel what Robbie felt. This man had hunted Baldur. He wanted to return him to the nightmare world of the animal house. And now he threatened the person Baldur valued above all others. Rage boiled up inside Robbie's head, alongside a hunter's cool calculation of weight and distance; of where to place first one foot, then the next.

"No!" Robbie struggled to damp down the overpowering emotion inside him. But it wasn't Baldur who lost control. Freya knew these people too. The tension of being this close to the ones who had removed her from the forests of her homeland and then locked her up in a box was more than she could endure. With an ear-piercing yowl not of fury, but of sheer terror, she launched herself across the bridge, heading for the security of the forest.

In her desperation to avoid Joe, she angled towards the side of the bridge, her heavy body colliding with Gavin Moir. As she hurtled past — intent only on gaining the freedom of the woods — he slithered wildly on the slippery cobbles, struggling to regain his balance as his feet slipped from under him and he pitched forward, over the parapet of the bridge.

Chapter 24

Robbie threw himself forward and grabbed at Moir's flailing hand. The man's other hand slammed down on the slippery stones and he hung there, suspended over the drop, while Robbie's muscles screamed at the effort of holding on to a full-grown man.

But Baldur could not understand what Robbie was doing. This man had imprisoned and tormented him. Like Freya, he had no intention of ever being caged again. His mind drilled into Robbie's, urging him to let go, to finish it and let Moir fall to the rocks far below.

"No!" screamed Robbie, feeling the man's hand crush his own, the fingers slowly slipping away until at last, Moir's feet found the rough stone on the underside of the bridge and the pressure on Robbie's arm suddenly eased.

But Moir did not let go. He stared up at Robbie with grim determination. There was something there that Robbie had never seen before in a person. He was viewed as something that did not deserve to live, that should never have been born.

And now Moir had a chance to put things right. Robbie heard the sound of running feet — Joe and his father. But they would be too late. Moir weighed at least twice as much as he did. One little tug and it would be Robbie who fell. A tragic accident. With a terrible blinding clarity, Robbie understood that he was about to die.

He strained backwards, terror giving him a strength he had never known. He groaned in pain as he felt the bone in his shoulder slip out of its socket. And still inch-by-inch, he was moving forward, his feet sliding across the cobbles towards the edge of the bridge.

And then something huge and heavy inserted itself in the space between their outstretched arms. Robbie slammed against a warm, furry body and heard Gavin Moir let loose an agonised shriek. With a suddenness that sent Robbie tumbling to the ground, Moir let go.

"Robbie? Robbie! Are you all right?" His father's voice sounded panicky.

He looked up to see Baldur crouched on the parapet, all his fur standing on end, his snarling face inches from that of the man who clung to the stones with one arm, staring in disbelief at the blood welling up from the jagged holes in his sleeve.

I will not kill. It wasn't really a statement. Baldur was rigid with the effort of controlling his desire to rid himself of his tormentor. But Robbie had tried to save this man's life. The cat's mind was a dizzying turmoil of conflicting emotion.

Through the haze of pain, Robbie tried to send the message that the death of a human being would not go unpunished. If Baldur wanted to live, then he had to let Moir go. Baldur swung his head towards Robbie, then back to the man. Robbie held his breath.

After what felt like an eternity, the cat turned away and dropped to the cobbles. Robbie staggered to his feet with his father's help, cradling his injured arm. Michael was staring at Moir in furious disbelief.

"You nearly killed him!" He strode forward, his jaw clenched, hands reaching out like claws, but Robbie reached out with his good hand and caught his arm. "Dad, no."

"Don't be such a fool," snapped Moir, struggling to climb back on to the bridge. "I wasn't going to hurt him."

Michael started forward again, but Joe moved neatly between him and the object of his fury, hauling Moir roughly back across the parapet.

"This has gone far enough, Gavin." Joe's voice was hard. "And it's pointless anyway. I've already done what Michael asked. The samples are gone. Without them — and me — you've got nothing."

Moir glared at him as he pulled a handkerchief from his pocket and struggled to tie it round his arm. No one made any move to help him. "I've still got the cats."

He finished with his makeshift bandage and set off for the Land Rover. Robbie remembered the tranquillizer gun. He struggled desperately to keep the thought from Baldur, who was watching Moir with a feral gleam in his eye, all his instincts urging him to deal with the threat in the only way he knew.

"No, Gavin," called Joe. "You haven't got the cats. Don't you remember? They died. Some kind of virus, I think." He popped another piece of gum in his mouth. "I can check if you like. It's all on record back at the Institute."

Moir stopped walking. Slowly, he turned to face Joe. "You have no idea what you are doing," he said heavily.

"I think I do," said Joe. "And if I were you, I'd be very sure that if anything ever happens to Robbie, I'll know where to look."

Moir stared at him for a long moment, then he set off once more for the land rover. He pulled the door open and climbed into the passenger seat, still clutching his bleeding arm.

"I wish you had trusted me with the truth," Joe said to Michael. "If you had, then none of this would have happened."

Michael placed a protective arm around his son. "Maybe you're right," he said. "There were too many secrets. And too many lies. But at least Robbie is still here, with me. I have to thank you for that."

Joe grinned. "No need to feel too grateful. Baldur is no use to me anyway. You know as well as I do that an experiment is no use if it can't be repeated. I'll have to start again. And this time, I won't be using Jane's samples." He smiled at Robbie. "I'm truly sorry about all this." He held out a hand. "What do you say? Apology accepted?"

Robbie looked at the hand, then glanced over at Baldur, now calmly washing his face. Without Joe, Baldur never would have been born. He owed him for that, at least. But still, somehow, it took quite an effort to reach out and shake his hand.

Joe understood. "Fair enough," he said. "I don't suppose I'll be seeing you again." He grinned. "But

I'll know you're out here somewhere. You and the cats. Good luck to you, Robbie."

Robbie nodded and watched him walk away. He leaned into his father, careful of his sore shoulder. Joe climbed into the Land Rover, started the engine and disappeared with a farewell wave, Gavin Moir a silent, brooding presence beside him.

"What do you think?" Michael asked. "Is it time to go home? We'll need to get a doctor to look at your arm, though."

Baldur stood up and moved closer, butting his head against their legs. Robbie felt his father stiffen beside him.

"It's all right, Dad," he said gently. "It looks like Baldur has finally decided to trust you."

He smiled down at Baldur. "Looks like the good guys won this time, doesn't it?"

Baldur's emerald eyes glinted up at him.

Epilogue

Callum hurried uphill, his shoulders hunched, anxious to get out of the cold and the rain. He reached the cave and stopped at the entrance, frowning down at the pack lying at his feet. It hadn't been there when he left. He stood for a long time, wary and indecisive, before he grabbed it and hurried inside.

Kneeling beside the fire, he hummed to himself as he unpacked the bag: socks and gloves, a woolly hat and a set of thermal underwear. Below the clothes he found packets of flour, rice, dried noodles and vegetables ... and a large box of matches. Right at the bottom, there was an envelope with two words on it.

Thank you.

He tore open the envelope and pulled out a crisp, new, ten-pound note. He smiled. So the boy had made it after all.

Author's Note

Hox genes really do exist and they do control growth within the body. As for the rest, when I came across an article on the web about how ancient mammals had more Hox genes than they do now, it set me wondering ... What if those Hox genes were reintroduced? It was that "what if" that made me write this story.